JIM HARRISON

•

A GOOD DAY TO DIE

Delta
Trade Paperbacks

A DELTA/SEYMOUR LAWRENCE BOOK
Published by

A DELTA/SEYMOUR LAWRENCE BOOK
Published by
Dell Publishing
a division of
Bantam Doubleday Dell Publishing Group, Inc.
1540 Broadway
New York, New York 10036

ISBN: 0-385-28343-1 (previously ISBN: 0-440-53000-8)

Reprinted by arrangement with the author

Printed in the United States of America

LSI 001

BVG

A GOOD DAY
TO DIE

BOOKS BY JIM HARRISON

Fiction
WOLF
A GOOD DAY TO DIE
FARMER
LEGENDS OF THE FALL
WARLOCK
SUNDOG
DALVA
THE WOMAN LIT BY FIREFLIES
JULIP

Poetry
PLAIN SONG
LOCATIONS
OUTLYER
LETTERS TO YESENIN
RETURNING TO EARTH
SELECTED & NEW POEMS
THE THEORY AND PRACTICE OF RIVERS & OTHER POEMS

Nonfiction
JUST BEFORE DARK

to
DAN GERBER

AUTHOR'S NOTE: Certain technical aspects of the handling of explosives have been deliberately altered and blurred to protect innocent life and property.

Each torpid turn of this world bears such disinherited children
to whom neither what's been, nor what is coming, belongs.
                                                    —RILKE

PART
I

PROLOGUE

DOUBLE-ANCHORED off Cudjoe Key: barely dawn and she's still asleep but I was awakened by water birds. So many. The first sight upward from the skiff's bottom was an osprey with a small snake hanging from her talons—back to the nest now in the rookery for breakfast. Almost chilly, in the mid-sixties at six A.M., but it will be eighty by noon. I wanted to get over to the Snipe Key basin and catch the incoming tide and what fish would be there looking off that huge sandspit toward the rank mangroves. She's snoring, when she said she'd never sleep as the boat's bottom was too hard and we had no air mattresses. Drone of a sponger off to work. How they stand in that narrow prow without falling off and it must be genetic. I talked to one for a half hour once and understood nothing. She's waking. Lukewarm coffee in the Thermos. The mosquitoes were bad in the night and sand fleas. Over the freeboard I see a small sand shark nuzzling around the prongs of the sea anchor.

"Let's go back," she says.

"I thought you wanted to fish."

"That was the margaritas you gave me."

I thought for a moment of kicking her ass out of the boat but that would be murder. We were sweating like piggies in that sleeping bag and I thought how in youth I had heard about our soldiers in the Orient getting rolled up in rugs with Chinese girls. Too hot and we didn't manage. After coming out at dusk with the markers not totally visible. Only a drunk or a master would try it and I was the former. I stood on the freeboard and cast a streamer but a barracuda snipped the leader when he struck.

I watched her dress with no interest. No panties, only white bells and a muslin blouse under which her breasts swung free and that was why I asked her out here. But she grew progressively dense after so much laughter. I tied on another tippet and small keel hook streamer. There is a long happy streak when half drunk: everything is possible on earth—love, sanity, enormous fish, fame. I met her in Captain Tony's, a saloon off Duval. A dozen drinks and some shrimp and picadillo in a Cuban restaurant. Then borrowed a friend's boat and took off from Garrison Bight with beer and a pint and a Thermos of coffee, some bread and cheese. I only stopped off Cudjoe because of darkness. I popped a beer; my head ached insanely and I wanted fresh water and aspirin but we had none.

"My friends will worry about me."

"Your friends won't be up for a few hours."

I pulled the anchors and coiled the dripping rope. She chewed on the bread and drank out of the Thermos, shivering. I checked the gas. The tank was nearly full but then I remembered Felipe had filled it while we bought the beer. I turned on the marine radio and picked up a Havana station which was playing some wild Latin music. I thought it would cheer her up. I checked the lower unit then pressed the powertilt and started the motor. Birds flew up by the thousands from a small key a hundred yards away. A few roseate spoonbills among them.

"Don't go fast, it will make me colder," she said over the

idling motor. It would be nice to drag her by an anchor rope at forty knots. I pointed toward Snipe Key and accelerated.

"You're going the wrong way," she shouted.

"A shortcut." I intended to have a look at the basin if it meant binding and gagging her. I slowed down enough to reach for the chart under the seat so I could check for the markers. They are generally easy to see, with a cormorant perched on each one.

"Why don't you get back in the bag?"

She looked at me quizzically then crawled in. If the water had been choppy she would have been pounded senseless. I pushed the throttle up to full bore, covering the seven miles flat out at forty knots, but when I pulled up to the basin the water was too shallow to enter. I got out the tide book to see if the wait would be long but the book was inscrutable. Numbers. I looked at the far end of the basin through my binoculars to see if any bonefish were tailing but the water was flat and motionless.

"Why did you stop?" she asked, peeking out of the bag.

"So I wouldn't tear out the fucking lower unit."

"Don't get mad."

"We don't have enough water to get over the reef."

"Can we turn around?" She was sniffling now, in part from her obvious hangover. She looked at me as if I were a madman, not altogether inaccurate as a judgment of character. It is hard enough to wake up in a motel room with a woman you don't really know. I began to try to remember her last name but drew a blank. Ansel. Atkins. Aberdeen. Angus. Cow. There was nothing to do but turn around and head back to Key West. I eased the boat around at low throttle in the shallow water, disturbing a small, beautiful leopard ray.

"Where are we going now?"

"The Japs have closed off the channel. Keep your head down."

Now her eyes were truly fearful. No gift for the surreal, a dull stenographer's brain.

"Have a beer," I suggested.

"I'd throw up."

The questioning eyes again, reminding me of a retarded collie pup I owned as a boy. Bit a bicycle tire and caught its teeth in the wire spokes. Back broken when flipped. How I mourned for puppies.

"You look like a puppy I owned once."

She made another snivel noise and receded into the sleeping bag. A giant turd. Burial at sea. I'll play taps on the kazoo when I dump the bag over. Full throttle again, following the markers to Key West, singing fly the friendly skies of united over the motor whine. Jingo songs stick in my head. Do all people sing when alone in their cars? Once in Boston I was bellowing out Patsy Cline's "The Last Word in Lonesome Is Me" and at a stoplight a truck driver clapped.

I entered Key West channel at full speed passing the Navy officers' housing with a sign of NO WAKE tacked to each dock. An early morning wake for each. A dawn riser stood on his lawn and mouthed a soundless "slow down" and I gave him the finger.

At the marina Felipe looked at us and said a pleasantry in Spanish while tying up the boat.

"Dumbo cunto stupido no fisho," I said pointing at my mate who was crawling out of the bag. Felipe giggled.

We drove in silence down Duval to the Pier House where she was staying. She got out and flounced to the motel door without a backward glance. Oh well.

CHAPTER

1

I WENT BACK to my room and lolled around naked. I took a shower and examined my insect bites and my gritty bloodshot eyes. Was it all worth it? No. The soul of a clerk bent deeply over his arithmetic. Eve proffers the clerk an apple which turns out to be hollow and contains a howling succubus. I considered smoking a little dope but rejected the idea—after a nap I wanted to play pool and dope always took the edge off whatever competitive spirit I had left in the world. Stretched out on the cot my thoughts alternated between pool and fishing in an attempt to rid my brain of the girl. She would be in a perfect snit by now. Perhaps it had happened a hundred times. The clerk again. Maybe only seventy-seven. A rack of pool balls lay gleaming against green felt. The one-ball is yellow but then the color of the two-ball escaped me. The water was calm and very clear and shallow and some maniacs could see tarpon coming a quarter of a mile away. They would deliver their casts with graceful fluid motions while I would chop the air in panic. In Ecuador the Indian mate was too poor to buy Polaroid glasses but he saw the caudal fins of marlin long before my perfect eyes noticed anything. Benny played pool as if the cue stick emerged from his body. Not my own alcohol and geometry. She was an asshole and I couldn't have loved her at gun point.

The late afternoon sun flowing in a sheet through the window. Why didn't I draw the blinds. Sweating with the air apparently the same temperature as my blood's. I dressed quickly in a light khaki shirt and suntans and tennis shoes. Anonymity. I took a beer from my boat cooler but the ice cubes had melted and the beer was lukewarm. I drank it looking out at the white hotness of Duval Street. The world looked askew and foreign. The girl might be just getting up from an air-conditioned nap, stretching her admittedly attractive limbs and deciding to be more careful about whom she left bars with.

In Sloppy Joe's I drank three or four glasses of beer waiting for a used-car salesman from Denton, Texas, to show up. We played pool nearly every afternoon when I got through fishing and he finished hustling sailors into car deals they couldn't afford. I was pleased with the way beer made me feel like an ordinary sot. Maybe I was really a veteran or a pipefitter or carpenter. Seventh Airborne or something like that. After a case of Budweiser I might have voted for Goldwater. A retired chief petty officer, a passing acquaintance, sat down next to me and began rattling off complaints about the weather, his car, his wife's drinking, and then politics. When drunk he was not above trying to run over a hippie. I had once teased him about the Navy's combat readiness at Pearl Harbor and that after that debacle they were lucky to get their hands on a rowboat. He was on the verge of hitting me but I apologized and bought him several drinks.

The car salesman finally came in and we played a nearly wordless hour of eightball during which I lost twelve dollars. I won five of it back playing nineball but then he left saying that the "little woman" would have dinner ready. I had a disturbing image of a female midget before a stove stirring food with teeny-weeny hands. I went back to a stool at the bar and ordered a double bourbon straight up. I was tired of going to the bathroom every fifteen minutes to get rid of the beer. I glanced out through the large open doors to see if anyone interesting was wandering around but it was the dinner hour lull and dusk still came rather early in April. Then I noticed that there was a strange-looking guy sitting directly across the circular bar staring at me. He was large with fairly long hair, tanned and extremely muscular with a small eagle tattooed on his left forearm. But the right side of his face was distorted with a bleached twist of scar tissue and it drew his eye a few degrees off center. I instantly averted my glance. Perhaps a shrimper and they're always cutting each other up.

"What are you staring at?"

"Nothing. I was looking over your head at the street." Shot of adrenaline. A single drop of sweat moved down the inside of my leg.

He turned around and looked out the open door behind him and I drew in my breath. Then he swiveled quickly on his stool and stood up. "How about a game?"

"O.K."

He flipped me a quarter for the rack and walked over to the jukebox. By the time he chose his cue Jim Ed Brown had started singing "Morning," a song I rather liked about country style adultery. Who screws who in Mingo County. It seemed to me that you had to be out in the country, traveling, or rather drunk to listen to such music.

"Eightball for a buck?"

"Fine with me."

He broke very hard and got two stripes and a solid but I quickly saw on the next shot that he was a slammer, a hard stroker who didn't play for shape. This sort of player can be very accurate but he plays with his balls, his manhood, and never leaves himself well for the next shot except by accident: a pointless arrogance, a kind of dumbbell "macho." His speech was Southern, either Alabama or Georgia, without the singsong effect you hear in Mississippi. While he shot I thought of a record a teacher had played for us in college with Faulkner talking about fox hunting. The record was studiously fatuous with the great man's voice high pitched and lacking the timbre one would imagine in his heroes, say Bayard Sartoris.

I won a half dozen games in a row but he was only mildly irritated. He drew the money out out of a bulky clip. There were twenties and fifties in quantity and I wondered idly why anyone would take the chance. But then I thought that it was unlikely that anyone would attack him.

"My muster pay." He had read my thoughts.

"Vietnam?"

"A year and a half's worth."

Now two sailors were watching us play, obviously sizing up our game for a challenge. One of them was small and wiry and was giggling while the other who was large and beefy merely stared. Then the big one put a quarter on the edge of the table which meant he was challenging the winner. I had just missed an easy shot and was irritable. It was bad etiquette to put a quarter up while someone was shooting. My partner took the quarter and deftly flipped it out into the street where it rolled rather electrically in a small circle. I held my breath.

"What are you, a smartass?" the big sailor said. My partner continued his shooting but then the sailor picked up the eightball and dropped it in a pocket. "That ends your game, smartass."

I felt a touch of vertigo and moved instinctively toward the door but curiosity stopped me. I couldn't see any sign in my partner's face of what he was going to do except that he chewed his gum more rapidly. He looked down at his left hand which held the cue stick and then at his right which was empty. Then with startling speed he clouted the sailor in the ear with the heel of his hand. The arc of the swing was wide but fast and the sailor collapsed on his butt with a yelp. There was a quick boot to his chest and then the cue stick pressed across his throat until he began to gag. I saw the other sailor looking at me but he only shrugged. Several barflies had gathered around us.

"We're playing pool now. When we're done you can play." He was letting his full weight rest on his knee on the sailor's chest. Then he stood abruptly and the sailor stumbled to the door.

"Those fucking creeps think they own this town." Now he was smiling and we sat back down at the table but the bartender was standing next to us.

"You guys are cut off."

"You don't know what those guys said." I found myself talking. "They said we were queers and we weren't allowed in the bar. Do we look like queers to you? What if someone called you a queer?"

The bartender paused, trying to figure out if I was bullshitting him, but then the chief petty officer who was now terribly drunk said he had heard the whole thing. We were allowed to stay and I gave the chief the victory sign and ordered him a drink. We played another game of pool but lost interest.

"What if that guy had known karate?"

"Nobody knows karate if you get a good one in first." He laughed and put another quarter in the jukebox.

We began drinking steadily and talked about everything excluding the war: baseball (Boog Powell who played for the Orioles was from Key West), music, fishing, the girls that now walked by the door with splendid regularity. Many of the girls were tourists or college girls down for Easter week but some were local conchs and Cubans. He liked the Cubans but I preferred the tourists as I considered Latin girls to be somewhat frightening and unreliable. For an instant I thought of the girl I had met the evening before—all that I had drunk made her seem interesting again. He said that his name was Tim and that he was from Valdosta, Georgia, and was staying a few weeks on Stock Island with his sister who was married to a Navy man he described as a "real jackoff." We were getting fairly drunk and I wanted something to eat before I lost control. We quarreled mildly about whether a pump or a double-barreled shotgun was better for bird shooting. I really wanted to ask him about the war but felt afraid to bring it up.

"I never ate in a French restaurant." He was looking over my shoulder at the only one in town. "Are we dressed up enough?"

"I've been in there. It costs a lot."

"I'll buy. I won a lot of this at poker in the hospital."

"How long were you there?"

"Two months."

This was the first reference to his face. It was sort of a mess at close range and I wondered why the Army hadn't done plastic surgery.

"I'm not going back to the hospital," he said, anticipating my question.

He asked me what I was doing in town and I said that I came every year for a month or two to fish. I rambled on about the fishing and admitted that it seemed that every year I became less capable at it to the point that I dreaded going out with those who fished well. I said that it had always struck me that unless you were able to become single minded about fishing and hunting you would fail. You were either obsessive and totally in control or you were nothing. He didn't appear interested in these subtleties. I suddenly thought that it would be fun to kick the shit out of someone in a few seconds, which was obviously one of his talents. I reflected on all the multifoliate ways you parry when you first meet someone.

When we got up to leave I noticed for the first time that the eagle on his tattoo had a beak that was drawn up into a maniacal smile and asked him about it.

"Just a joke to piss people off."

"They're going to dam up the Grand Canyon," I said halfway across Duval Street. Tim stopped and looked at me, puzzled. A car beeped.

"You're shitting me."

"Nope."

We entered the resturant and the hostess with a quick knowing glance seated us in a corner as far from other customers as possible.

"Where'd you hear about that?" he said looking at the menu.

"I read about it. It's true." For a moment I had been lost. It had only been an errant comment.

"No kidding?"

"Word of honor," I said raising my two fingers in a mock cub scout sign.

"Jesus Christ, it will fill up with water." He was clearly troubled and I wanted to drop the subject.

I ordered drinks from the waiter who was obviously a homosexual. He raised his eyebrows at me as if I had scored and I was terribly embarrassed. But then I supposed that we didn't look like we quite fit together. Some homosexuals have an uncanny ability to figure people out by their immediate appearances.

"I don't understand this shit. You order for us."

I asked for two orders of steak au poivre and some endive, which seemed inoffensive. Then the waiter asked us if we wanted wine.

"Yeah, I want some fucking champagne," Tim said a bit loudly but the waiter was charmed.

We got out of the place with difficulty. The food was excellent, especially the endive which reminded me of New York, but the waiter tried to clip us when he returned the change. We had had a half dozen cups of Cuban coffee which had a nerve-jangling effect mixed with all the pepper and alcohol. The owner placated us at the door with assurances that it wasn't intentional on the waiter's part but I felt very melancholy pondering all the little cheats people pull on one another. Up on Big Pine Key a wealthy angler from Vermont had tried to cheat on a fishing record by filling the gullet of a bonefish with sinkers. He had bribed his guide to go along with the little project. A gesture at a corner of immortality and not at all concomitant with what you thought of the stern Yankees. Meanwhile the waiter was standing sullen in the background.

"You ought to fire that cocksucker," Tim said loudly.

"Let's go." I pulled on his arm. His word had had a magical effect on the restaurant. We were being looked at in mute wonderment. I waved and grinned at some people I knew. I wanted to leave before the owner called the police. The local police were very authoritative. A few nights before I had seen one dragging a shrimper from a bar by the hair and the shrimper's eyes were buggy with pain. I was somehow sure that Tim wouldn't react gracefully to such treatment.

CHAPTER

2

We walked around the corner and into Captain Tony's, which was dark and crowded. Behind the dancing area a jug band was playing and a guy with a pigtail was singing loudly and not very well. We moved down the length of the bar and sat near the pool table and jukebox.

"I wish I had one."

"One what?" It was hard to hear over the music. I tried to signal the barmaid.

"A pigtail."

"You're putting me on." This was a surprise—my ordinary conception of a Georgia cracker involved shooting treed blacks or messing around with old cars, though as time passed it seemed much easier for a black to get himself shot in Detroit than anyplace else. "You could grow one."

"How long would it take?"

"Don't know. Never grew one."

He was becoming plaintive and morose about the prospect of waiting for a pigtail. The barmaid came and I ordered two beers. She looked bored but took an unusual interest in Tim which made me slightly jealous as I had never been able to gather her attention. Tony always hires the most beautiful barmaids in Key West and the Navy pilots come in numbers, fall in love and are rejected. The barmaids, it seems, are in love with musicians and other worthless types who wear pigtails and are always broke. The barmaids are not interested in sleek pilots with thin mustaches and wallets full of flight pay. When the blond one whose name was Judy bent over the cooler to get our beer we were cleanly mooned. Polka-dot panties. But I knew she was hopeless because she lived with a rather affable freak who sold tacos from a pushcart.

I realized we had become less drunk and would have to start over again, a practice that is known as a double-header. I had clearly peaked out and was on my way down. I could scarcely swallow the beer, my head ached and I wanted a nap, full dress and under the covers. By myself. All the pepper on the steak had given me heartburn and I needed some Gelusil.

"That's really true?" Tim was staring into my eyes.

"What?"

"About the Grand Canyon?"

"It's at least in the planning stage." Now I truly regretted saying anything.

"I've never seen the Grand Canyon."

I was on the verge of saying it was very large then giggled at the idea. I had seen Glen Canyon years ago before it was literally drowned and liked it better but any comparison was absurd with such splendors. And besides I was a Chicken Little and tended to believe in nonsense. I had once read in a New York underground newspaper that an asteroid was going to hit Long Island Sound and the resultant tidal wave would kill everyone. I sat in our little apartment in Port Jefferson and brooded about the logic and scientific probabilities involved. I convinced my wife and she had nightmares of burning railroad cars and bloated sheep. When the appointed day went by without a single asteroid I was embarrassed.

"We probably ought to blow up the goddamn thing." Tim nodded in assent then spoke but I couldn't hear him over the band. I suddenly felt very bored and claustrophobic. "I got to go."

"Why? We're just getting started."

"I'm tired and I have to be up at six tomorrow to fish."

"I'll fix you up." He began searching his pockets then stood and looked blankly at me. "Ride with me to my sister's. I got some uppers."

I hesitated, weighing alternatives. Did I want to get blasted? If I did I wouldn't go fishing in the morning. With a hangover a two-foot chop sends me puking despite Merazine. Probably be too windy anyway—I had noticed the palms swaying on the side street. And maybe this guy was crazy too. I hadn't envied the sailor. I didn't like the idea of dropping speed with alcohol in my guts. Blood pressure soars. I looked at my watch—only nine o'clock—and remembered how much I had always disliked people who copped out on a good drunk. You would just get started talking and laughing and playing pool and they would go home to their wives. Pussy-whipped we called it. I couldn't go home to my wife. Six months now.

"Let's hear the rest of the set first." The jug band was getting better. A tall black woman was singing a Joplin tune, a graceful reverse gesture. She was well over six foot and wore a white silk sheath dress that allowed her hip bones to protrude. She was awesome.

"God I'd like some of that," Tim said.

I nodded agreement but admitted to myself that I wouldn't dare try it. Now that I had decided to stick it out the beer went down easily and I thought how deftly the brain screws up the stomach and breathing. We played a few games of nineball for five dollars and I lost them all.

"You can owe me," he said.

I checked my wallet. I had two hundred back in the room but had to make it last. I put twenty-five dollars in my pocket each morning and stuck to this budget. I had nearly run out of people to borrow from. The liquor was obviously bothering my shooting more than his. It was between sets and the jukebox was playing a Beatles tune that had a phrase "we all shine on." I liked the music but the lyrics were so patently absurd. How like me to be questioning the rock lyrics when I should have been concentrating on pool. There goes the allowance.

"Let's go get that shit and come back."

Tim drove very fast but capably down the back streets until we caught Route 1 for the short trip to Stock Island. A Detroit jockey, a Dodge with four on the floor. His sister lived in a large mobile home and was watching the tube when we entered. *Marcus Welby, M.D.* She was frowsy and dilapidated, perhaps ten years older than Tim.

"Pleased to meetcha," she said without getting off the couch. I sat and watched the Doctor with her while Tim went in the other room. It seems the Doctor was telling a young woman that her husband had to have a kidney transplant and they couldn't afford it. Her eyes flickered moistly as did Tim's sister's. Commercial. The room smelled of fried potatoes.

"Where you from?" she said turning from the set.

"Michigan."

"My husband he's from Flint. He's in Pensacola for a few days. Want a beer?" She was drinking hers straight from the can.

"No thanks."

Tim came in with a bottle of pop.

"Offer your friend a Coke, Timmy." The commercial was

over and she was watching Marcus as he strode resolutely across a hospital parking lot.

"No. We're going. See you later."

"Be careful," she said.

I had been staring at a lamp in the corner that had a black plaster leopard as its base. From the leopard's skull protruded the stem and bulb and shade. The leopard had green pastel eyes and painted white snarling teeth and a chipped jaw.

When we got into the car he handed me two spansules which I dropped with a swig of pop. He dropped four.

"You're going to fuck up your head."

"Right," he said.

On the way back downtown we talked about college which I couldn't remember very well. He said that he had gone to Georgia Tech for two years before dropping out and enlisting. It wasn't too hard but it was boring and there had been too few cunt around the place. He had re-upped after his first year in Vietnam to get the extra volunteer pay and to avoid marriage. He thought he had got his girl pregnant but then she miscarried. It somehow sounded old fashioned.

We pulled up near Tony's and it was even more crowded than before. I talked to a head I knew vaguely and he gave me directions for a party on Sugarloaf Key after the bar closed. The speed had already taken effect and my system was winding up like a jet engine. I felt young and stupid. Tim looked calm enough though his eyes were a bit glittery. We bought drinks for two college girls from Ohio and asked them if they wanted to go to a party. They were suspicious. Too straight. And I was twenty-eight, clearly not a college student, and Tim's scar didn't seem to help.

"Why don't you go home and play with each other. See if we give a shit," he said. They were startled and moved quickly to the far end of the bar. Then we asked a hip-looking girl with long blond hair if she wanted a drink and she accepted and when we mentioned a party she said she already knew about it but would ride with us. She recognized me from the Cuban diner where I ate regularly. I was disappointed—she was vacant and simple-minded—but Tim was enthralled. A fat soiled-looking girl approached and our new friend offered her a ride. She was homely but her brain was absolutely vivacious compared to the beauty who kept saying she was "strung out" as if the condition were unique on earth.

On the way out to Sugarloaf Key we passed around several bombers that Tim took from under the dashboard. The grass was Colombian buds, dry and hot and powerful. I entered some sort of fantasy time warp where I was out on the flats at noon repeating and perfecting every bad cast I had made in five years. I now felt that my brain was a purring electric motor and that my fingers would fry people at touch. Usually with drugs there was a small undisturbed center in my brain that could view what was happening with clarity. But it had been swallowed by the unilaterally manic notion that my whole body was less than an inch thick and the only backing I had on earth was the back seat of a car. Now the warm air coming in the window reminded me of a thousand other summer nights and I was dazed and constricted. The fat girl began humming. I thought in self-defense of the pleasant time I had had when I dropped four hits of psilocybin, lay down in a creek for an hour and became a trout. An infatuation with poisons.

We pulled into a yard after some confused circling. The subdivision roads were made of crushed coral and the noise of the tires was nearly unbearable. It was a small place built on the principle of stilts in anticipation of tropical storms, with the lower half of the house given over to a utility room and a screened-in area and the upper half containing kitchen and bedrooms, the functional living space. The house abutted a canal; I knew you could go out the canal and through Tarpon Creek to get to the Gulf Stream or Loggerhead Key. The shrubbery was dense and there were about a dozen cars. The music was very loud and when we entered people seemed sprayed about everywhere in a semi-comatose state. I went upstairs to the kitchen and drank a lot of lukewarm water from the tap. All water is piped from the mainland but I didn't want to snoop in their refrigerator for the water bottle even in my advanced state of looniness. A group was sitting at the kitchen table talking intently and passing a joint. Smelled strange, perhaps laced with something. I went back downstairs looking for Tim but couldn't find him. Then I went outside to muffle the music a bit and some people were swimming beneath a dim boathouse light. The light attracted an enormous swarm of insects some of which looked as large as sparrows. I shed my clothes and jumped into the warm brackish water. No sharks I hoped but they rarely come into the canals: out on the flats at night tearing into mullet or anything that moves. I hung in the water, my hand grasping a tire that served as a boat buffer; dizzy, weightless, joyless. The pretty girl was next to me but her face was flat as a magazine cover. I reached out and touched her. She began giggling and I became more conscious though it was apparent that my body was made of rubber, an extension of the tire I held on to. I felt her sex, slippery in the water, and she squeezed her eyes shut. I held my breath and sank into the water and began nuzzling her but it required too much effort. She climbed up the ladder and I followed, a dazzling sight. We gathered our clothes and walked through the bushes to Tim's car and got into the back seat still wet with salt water. She took a joint from her purse and I lit it taking only two drags as I was so spaced I was sure the car was moving. Vague taste of hash. A single mosquito. I began kissing her again and she dropped the roach out the window and returned the gesture. Skin sticking to the Naugahyde with the glue of wet salt. But I was a small motor again, metallic. Part of my brain thought of my wife and how we hid behind sexuality when nothing else worked. Saline. Aqueous. I watched my lower half drift out to sea.

3

WAKING. In a jumble. What noise was that? Tim's face framed in the car window. After dawn. My ear still against her thigh, my head light. Tim smoking a cigarette looked a trifle scary— the wound was more distinct when he was pale, fatigued. He stared at the sleeping girl, his head half in the window. Blond above and brown below. Trickery. I rubbed my face and extricated myself and her limbs were limp, unwaking. I took my clothes from the front seat and crawled out. Most of the cars were still there but covered with dew. I dressed and smoked a cigarette.

"You sure lucked out," Tim whispered, gazing at the girl.

"I didn't know she was that pretty." I tried very hard but couldn't remember anything pleasant except the flex of her butt when she climbed the ladder under the lamp with beads of water falling. And a generalized ache about home.

We walked toward the house. Tim said he had snorted a few lines of cocaine but it wasn't good. Then someone had put nearly a lid of Colombian in a huge waterpipe and people had become comatose. What joy. In the kitchen the fat girl we had given a ride to had made coffee and a pitcher of orange Kool-

Aid which I despised but drank anyway. It made one seven years old again. My mustache smelled of the sea.

"Where did you and Marilyn disappear to?" the fat girl asked.

"He was out getting protein." Tim laughed. I suspected he had dropped some more pills. Fingers drumming on the table, bouncing aimlessly around the room.

I went over to the sink and washed my face. The water even smelled bad. I took an ice cube out of the Kool-Aid and dropped it in my coffee letting the splash burn my hand. The first sensation of the day.

"Anyone going to Miami?" She had her back turned and was looking out the window at an egret that picked its way along the canal bank.

The question seemed to puzzle Tim. I was disoriented and Miami had sounded like a foreign country. Anyone going to Germany or Peru. A palmetto bug made its way across the floor and Tim stepped on it. A squishy crackling sound out of proportion to the bug's size.

"We're going to the Grand Canyon," he said.

I looked at Tim, thinking about the Grand Canyon and the motorcyclist who was supposedly going to fly across it. Evel Knievel was his name.

"You could get off at Coral Gables or Hialeah," he told her.

"How come you guys are going to the Grand Canyon?" Her eyes were opaque and rheumy. The air-conditioner whirred on. It would be a hot day.

"We're going to blow up the dam out there," Tim said matter-of-factly as if the dam were to be equated with the palmetto bug.

"Oh." She paused. "Groovy."

I saw a mushroom cloud and turbulent water crashing and pouring through rubble. And men running like ants around the ruins of a huge dam. The valley would be flooded and people

perish. Walter Cronkite would give it half the evening news
time. And there would be an extra news special with the holo-
caust looked at from many angles. The ground, a heliocopter,
a Cessna. Then I remembered mentioning it in passing the
night before.

The heads began filtering into the kitchen, my saltine lover
among them. She smiled. Tim began running around the
kitchen yelling boom boom boom.

"These guys are going out West to blow up a dam," the fat
girl said. We were looked at with a mixture of admiration and
sleepy shock.

My system began to speed up in a rush, no doubt the leftovers of what I had been dropping and smoking, and I felt
preternaturally tough and gutsy, a little fated and doomed like
a samurai or some tropical exile holding dark secrets. My voice
became tight and humorless as I began a tirade against realtors, land developers and lumber companies. In a few years
there wouldn't be much worth looking at and if anyone in the
room planned on having a son there wouldn't be any rivers or
forests left and our sons wouldn't have any fishing and hunting.
What was needed was some sort of Irgun like the Israelis had
when they drove out the British. Some men brave enough to
blow up dams and machinery. Tim nodded and kept saying yes
and I felt encouraged though several of the heads had wandered out of the kitchen. I had become a battle- and grief-
hardened fighter for justice and momentarily wondered if any
of my little freak audience were government agents. Then my
lover left with her friends and my voice trailed off. Up and
down. Chemicals. The hero is abandoned with only the three
of us.

"When are you leaving?" The fat girl was distracted and intent upon her ride.

"I'm not going anyplace. I came down here to go fishing and
I'm going fishing." Out of the window the wind was rippling

the canal. I had heard that there was a front coming in from the northwest and wondered where I would find a lee to fish in for the next few days.

"Don't be such a chickenshit. Two days out and two days back and then you can fish."

I could see that Tim was buzzed up from my speech and excited about the idea of sabotage.

"If you don't go you're just another bullshitter." Now he had me in a corner and I felt silly and helpless.

"You can't drive to Arizona in two days." I felt myself weakening.

"We'll change off. We'll stop in Valdosta. I know a girl who will want to go. You'll really dig her."

Offering plums while I was trying to think clearly. Why not see the Grand Canyon. It was late April and early for the best tarpon fishing. We could eat some Mexican food. I was hungry and thought about all the Mexican dishes I liked.

"I don't have the bread."

Tim shrugged, patting his wallet pocket. His face brightened as I neared agreement.

My thinking became muddy and tenuous. Never been West by the Southern route and I always wondered flipping through the Rand-McNally what it looked like. Gumbo. Might take five days not four, or more assuming we might blow the engine, run into a tree or bridge abutment, or likely end up in jail somewhere with not enough money for bail. The prospect of jail food horrified me though I had only eaten in jail for two meals—concealed weapons, blackjack, charge in Duluth when I was sixteen—and it was oatmeal with powdered milk for breakfast and meatless beans at noon. And I feared disorientation. Back in the days of Thorazine . . . Those paralyzing anxiety attacks when the arms go numb, breathing is difficult, tunnel vision, feet won't move; the temporary incomprehension of things like shoes, hands, cars, buildings, as if you had just descended from Saturn and were looking at earth for the first time through the eyes and brain of some galactic foreigner, a lumpy space beast with atrophied sensors. I felt safe in three minimal areas of Michigan, Montana and Key West. Or pretty much in any woods or on any body of water. I read a true story of how Hölderlin, the German poet, was found standing in a nobleman's garden in the winter: a half foot of snow had gathered on his head and he was mistaken for a statue of Hölderlin. I thought I understood.

"O.K. but only five days on the outside."

"Let's go back to town and pick up our junk." Tim nodded and tucked in his shirt in mock readiness.

The next few hours proved bleary, exhausting. We promised the fat girl we would pick her up in an hour or so on our way back out from Key West. Then we drove into town with the sun glaring through the windshield, a humid morning with temperature near eighty by nine. I felt queasy and craved food and a pick-me-up, say a bloody mary or a stinger. Bad habit. All the garbage along Route 1 was supernaturally irritating. We passed an abandoned gas station where the week before coming back from Big Pine I had watched two girls fighting. They were about sixteen and one had the decided advantage of being able to punch like a male while the other was only capable of slapping. I parked until it aborted into a shrieking contest.

We went to my room first and Tim took a shower while I packed a few things in an overnight bag including bottles of various tranquilizers and vitamins and a four-piece fly rod I take everywhere with me because it breaks down into a handy two-foot tube. It occurred to me that I should question my motives but found that I had none. I took a shower when Tim got out. He was shirtless and I reflected while the hot water poured on my head that he had a rare physique: a mesomorph who gave the appearance of being constructed out of sloping fleshy cables and knots. I looked at my body in the mirror: about fifteen pounds overweight though I regularly exercised myself into a frazzle, like carrying two lake trout around my waist everywhere I went. I struck a bodybuilder pose and quacked loudly.

We ate a big Cuban breakfast, a steak with two fried eggs on it with raw onion, yellow rice and black beans, and I began to feel better about our little proposed adventure though I doubted the sensation would last. Tim was exultant and rattled on about cars, explosives, bird dogs and women. I allowed him to enviously assume that I had screwed the ears off the girl. We drove over to his sister's and I sat in the car fiddling with the radio knob. Sheriff Bobby Brown was talking about law and order. It was hot parked in the sun but Tim came out in a few minutes carrying a ratty duffel bag and wearing a newish pair of black tooled cowboy boots. His sister waved to me from the steps.

"Here we go." He gunned up the street leaving a thirty-foot stretch of rubber before he double-clutched into second, snapping my neck.

"You're out of your mind," I said.

Then I fell asleep, dreaming of motion, feeling a nudge as Tim removed a can of beer from my hand. A long bus trip with a stop in a small town in Kansas, a cafe with a lazy wood-paddled overhead fan. Acrid coffee at three A.M. Where was I going then, watching the warm black Kansas countryside pass the window with only a few barnyard lights? Dawn came on the other side of Topeka. A swig from the pint as it got lighter. Stretched out on the seat with a sweating forearm covering my eyes, a fifty-dollar bill in my sock so it wouldn't be stolen. Dizzy slow jolt of the bus hitting bumps and dips in the highway. Diesel fumes. Looking out the window at a stoplight in Denver downward into a car where a girl's dress was pulled upward to her waist as she waited for the green. Dreams of adventure, a fatal expectancy.

I awoke to a loudspeaker. We were in Islamorada at a drive-in and Tim was ordering some lunch into a black box. I smoked a cigarette, my mouth wretchedly dry and raw from last night's dope. A dowdy carhop who bounced rather than walked brought hamburgers with ketchup and mustard in small plastic containers that I couldn't seem to tear open. I drank some root beer and noticed Tim dropping two spansules with his. No more for me, ever. I turned around and looked at his duffel bag on the back seat.

"We forgot the girl."

"She'd stink up the car." He beeped and a different girl walked out lazily, a tanned teenage slattern barely more appetizing than lunch.

I thought of our fat friend. Maybe she didn't like showers but she was witty. What would she ever do but wait? And they always seemed to have urgent plans to go someplace whether it was Miami or New York or India. Often they owned small dogs. It is so much easier for the male to be homely. You see homely men with beautiful women but scarcely ever the reverse. Feckless. Early in college I had charmed a homely girl into writing papers for me in the two courses we shared, economics and natural science. But we occasionally went to the movies or had coffee and argued endlessly about Sartre and Camus who were all the rage then. So brilliant. She became a veterinarian at an amazingly accelerated rate. And went to Brazil to study parasites. She said in a card that Brazil was "delightfully wormy." Maybe she met a mad fucker down there for love after a hard day looking at tiny worms. Tape worms. I'm sort of homely but have given over thinking about it. I had a disturbing vision of taking a thousand fat girls to my kindly breast.

North out of Key Largo with vague thoughts of Humphrey Bogart's cancer. He wore the name very well. Such a long ride to go and Tim playing the maniac's part swooping out to pass when he probably shouldn't have. Another long doze and we were up near Fort Pierce and heading inland, wordless. By now I might have boated a bonefish or two but that was doubtful—staring out at the flats through the glitter of shallow water. And never growing bored with it. What else was there to do. Drink. Vote. Fall in love but I was most severely stricken by pictures of girls in magazines. I had written one, Lauren Hutton, a love letter which my wife had thought very funny.

We stopped near Ocala to get some beer and gas. It was purportedly nice country thereabouts but you couldn't see it because of all the billboards. I took over the driving so Tim could get some sleep but the car was too tight and muscular for my taste. I remembered a wonderful Model A I had owned as a teenager. I had bought it for fifty dollars from a retired farmer, retrieving it from a barn where it stood covered with hay chaff and swallow droppings. My dad started it with a crank and showed me how to hold the crank to avoid breaking my thumb when the engine kicked in. The Model A made a fine car for hunting and fishing—with its high axle clearance you could cover any terrain—and was more reliable than any car I had owned since. I tended to have personal feelings about my succession of used cars and was close to weeping when my '62 Ford Fairlane died on the Penn Turnpike. But Tim's car growled when the accelerator was depressed, understeered, was too aggressive, plus Tim was unable to sleep and watched my driving critically.

"This car is a pile of shit." I pitched my second empty over the seat. "How much did it cost?"

"Thirty-six hundred but I only made three payments."

I admired people who didn't co-operate with the economy. My own specious Calvinist breeding made me unable to cheat.

I was afraid someone would "get" me if I failed to pay the phone bill or the gas credit card. I was amazed when people I knew had a car repossessed and promptly went out and charged up another. Once I was a week late on a two-hundred-dollar note and a banker told me I was on the verge of ruining my credit. I had come into the bank with the money and he had lectured me at his desk about financial responsibility and how the economic health of the nation depended on the individual citizen. I blushed but stayed and took my "medicine."

"What if everyone refused to make car payments? The nation would be in a mess." I popped the last beer.

"Tough shit." He laughed. "Let's stop and get more beer and I'll drive. You're too slow." His eyes were a solid pink.

While Tim was getting the beer I looked around the parking lot of the party store. In front of an ice machine two attractive older women were talking in the evening light. And two cars over, three sunburnt men stood talking in summer suits. They looked a trifle criminal as if they had just stepped out of a John D. MacDonald novel. Realtors. When Tim walked out of the store whistling they stared at him sharply in unison but he was watching the women fiddle with their bags of ice.

We began talking about women but the talk immediately lapsed into sentimentalities. I described an idyllic affair I had had years before in Boston and became melancholy over the memory: the girl had terminated it mostly because she enjoyed living and had become disgusted with my tenacious self-pity. Tim spoke at length of Sylvia, the girl we would be seeing within a few hours. He had met her while still in high school and they had had an on-again, off-again relationship ever since. She had been very religious when he first noticed her, the sort of girl who had been raised a fundamentalist, belonged to the school Bible club, and went to church three times a week not counting the tent meetings when an itinerant evangelist would pass through Valdosta. But she was lovely and shy and he was a football player and was known to go to Atlanta whorehouses and race dirt-track stock cars on weekends. It had only taken a single evening at a drive-in for her to submit but then he began to love her and things had gone well for a few years though he refused to get married until he got the chance to "see the world." His time in Vietnam had changed things. When she visited him in the hospital in San Diego he still liked and wanted her but he had been through too much shit, too many drugs and Saigon whores for it to ever be quite the same again. She kept bringing up the idea of marriage until he became more and more abusive. It occurred to me that I had done something similar a number of times: you have ceased loving someone but you are still hanging on, so you begin to mistreat them.

The conversation took odd, beery turns: Tim talked of how the time drifted in the hospital and how on some days he would refuse medication to make sure he was alive. He said that when he was first wounded he thought he was dead and lay there waiting for something interesting to happen. Near the Florida-Georgia border he lost control, swerving and fish-tailing with all the empties clattering in the back seat to miss an opossum. We decided to stop and sleep off the beer.

CHAPTER

DRIVING down the main street at dawn, Valdosta still asleep and the trees leafy. Did General Sherman get this far? My little brother always lectured me on the Civil War as I was too lazy to read about it. We have very few magnolia in the north but I like their odor. The sun was orange over the cornices. Do they wear white linen suits with sweat rings. I was totally rested and wanted coffee. I looked at Tim and the whorl of scar tissue was shaped like a picture of a nebula, the knot in a white oak board. We stole white oak to build a Slocum boat, skidded it out of the woods with a Belgian mare in winter. Stored in a barn for seven years and no boat in sight. Around the world floating on stolen white oak. I wondered if the mare was dead. The theft was exciting; the land was owned by a Detroit dentist who only came up north once a year and we doubted that he would notice missing trees on five hundred acres. Then we stole his kennel. . . . We were driving past some row houses on a brick street, then past some houses with small neat yards. Flowering almond in many yards and wisteria.

"That's where I grew up."

Tim slowed the car. We were near the vaguely junky northern outskirts, still on a side street. The house was small and ramshackled and four cars were parked on the lawn.

"That old hemi-head Plymouth is my brother Verlin's."

I looked but I no longer recognized different cars. I nodded my head knowledgeably. Tim made a U-turn and speed-shifted into second, the tires making a helpless yelp and the engine roaring.

"Verlin will know that's me," he said chuckling.

We drove back toward the center of town and turned right onto a street of large houses which were once fine but now in disrepair. Almost daylight. I was tired of motion. He got out but I sat there a bit dazed.

"Come on. This is Sylvia's."

I followed him across the bare lawn and up the flimsy outside back stairs. He rattled the door violently. I heard the latch slip and a ponderous girl appeared. We walked in.

"This is Rosie."

I shook hands with her but the shades were drawn and the kitchen too dark to see clearly. There were the remnants of pizza on the counter and a bullfight poster over the sink. Bullfight posters even in Valdosta. Rosie flounced over to a daybed in what served as the living room.

"Timmy?" There was a girl standing in the bedroom door with a robe gathered around her. I couldn't see her clearly. Tim walked over and they closed the door.

"There's beer in the refrigerator," Rosie mumbled from her bed.

I stood looking out the kitchen window feeling the coldness inside my head, strangely suicidal. I had difficulty swallowing. Why am I here? Deranged again. How long has it been since I've been home? I thought of my little daughter in her Sunday frock skipping in errant circles around the yard. My dog. Would dog or daughter remember their father? A Valdosta back yard with a car up on blocks, the rear of a house just after dawn. Tears welled and were drawn back down by an uncertain will. How I've never committed an act without a consequent fuck-up. The point is to go whole hog I guess. Or to have a life like Tim's that is conceived and lived only in terms of the act. Dull thoughts. If you could figure it out you would still be in the kitchen with Rosie snoring over your shoulder. But I knew I could walk down the stairs, get my suitcase out of the Dodge, find the bus station and go back to Key West. And tomorrow at this time perhaps be out on Coupon Bight looking for the shadows of tarpon. Gliding over the skin of water. Roseate spoonbills and the three eaglets I saw eating rotten fish on a sandspit coming out of the mangroves. The sun blinding, the body in full sweat: sentient, casting the streamer above and ahead of the tarpon on an intercept pattern. Chokink again. I heard mumbling from the other room mixed with Rosie's snores. Lighter. I could see many beer cans and the used pizza was garish, the crust gone and the red sauce and solidified cheese looking like the leftovers of major surgery. Involuntary shudder. Near the breadbox was a half bottle of Beam. I took two burning gulps and a mouthful of beer to chase them. Morning. Where are the principles of order on earth? The whiskey's slow flushed rise up the spinal column.

Sylvia walked up behind me and as I turned she smiled. Almost a shudder. Tall and vaguely reddish hair, long and now in a single braid, perhaps for sleeping. Pale clear skin with a dust of freckles. Large hazel eyes. The old robe with an empire tuck at narrow high waist. Long legs. Nearly as tall as I am.

"You want coffee?"

"Please."

"Rosie's such a pig." She began cleaning up the kitchen. I

sat down at the table and watched her movements. She stooped to pick up a bottle top and I caught a flash and the outline of her thighs and butt. It was not so much the usual niggling desire and itch but as if I had caught some princess at her bath. This immediately increased my melancholy. She was Tim's not mine.

"I guess I'll go to the Grand Canyon with you guys." Her drawl was fainter than Tim's. She sat down across from me and I felt the blood rushing to my temples. "I don't like my job anyhow. I file insurance claims. I can't take shorthand or type very fast."

"I'm happy you decided to go." I looked at her eyes which were watching my hands clench on the table. "I think you'll like the Grand Canyon. You been there before?"

"I never been anywhere except Atlanta, and to Washington, D.C., once, and to San Diego to see Timmy." No self-pity here but modulated statement of fact. "How come you're drinking in the morning?"

I noticed I had put the Beam on the table along with my can of beer. Why was I drinking? I shrugged. "Don't know. Why not?"

Then she shrugged. "What's your job?"

"I'm on vacation." I felt uncomfortably on trial, the sweat beginning to emerge on my forehead. "Actually I've been out of work and work makes me vomit a lot so I want to stay out of work." Her eyes widened a bit and I was compelled to continue. "I've never found anything suitable, you know. So I borrow until I come across something I can do. I go fishing. Maybe you could call me a fisherman." The last said very loudly.

She looked at me quizzically. "That's no living. My dad went fishing too." She began to sound like my mother.

"You sound like my mother." She laughed then. "I'm twenty-eight and my mother sends me lots of advice."

Sylvia stood and went to the window. She scratched her leg idly. My stomach was upset from the whiskey and I wanted to crawl like a dog up behind her and nuzzle her ass.

"Timmy says you guys are going to blow up a dam in the Grand Canyon?" She turned. "I didn't know there was a dam there."

"Maybe there isn't." I had forgotten the supposed dam. "Maybe it's just on the drawing boards." I had an instantaneous sweeping fantasy of Sylvia in a log cabin in Montana late in the nineteenth century. It is May with only a few traces of snow left. She's in bed and has just died in childbirth; I've failed as a midwife. I gather the three children around me. The music will be Bill Monroe and his Bluegrass Boys singing "Mother's not dead, she's only asleepin' / Waiting patiently for Jesus to come." Her face would be beautiful but pale. The child was dead too. The kids pitched in and we buried her ten feet deep. With the baby on her breast.

"I know you'll get in trouble." I was brought back to earth. What was trouble anyway when your wife had just died. I wanted to take her in my arms now that she had been brought back to life. Rosie was at the refrigerator door gulping directly from a half-gallon carton of milk. I hadn't heard her get up. She looked at me with a dairy products mustache.

"You fuckoffs ought to be locked up." She giggled and began arranging bacon and eggs for breakfast. Then she popped a beer and drew heavily from the can. "Saturday morning I always have a beer," she said.

"In two swallows," Sylvia quipped.

"You're a candy ass." Rosie dumped a pound of bacon in the skillet and stirred it around over a high fire. Then she walked over to the phonograph and put on Buck Owens' Carnegie Hall album. Sylvia rolled her eyes in mock horror. Rosie sat leaning back on her chair to turn the bacon down. She poked

Sylvia in the ribs with a forefinger. "You're going along?" Sylvia nodded her head in affirmation. "Then Frank's going to stay with me."

Rosie began talking about Frank as she cooked breakfast. He had only been out of Raiford for three months. A stolen car charge and it seems he had some hot TV's in the trunk. She pulled open the silver drawer and drew out what she announced as Frank's Colt .38 and waved it around before handing it to me. Frank couldn't keep it because he was on parole. I snapped open the cylinder. Full. I pulled one cartridge and saw that he had scored the soft lead with a cross for the much admired dum-dum effect. A real hood. The bullet would blow a hole rather than puncture. Sylvia wasn't very attentive so Rosie dribbled a little cold beer from the can down her neck from behind.

She stood abruptly. "*Jesus!*" I saw one full wet breast as she dabbed it with a napkin. She was only vaguely embarrassed.

"Sylvia's proud of her knockers," Rosie said. Sylvia blushed deeply then. Why couldn't she be mine. Perhaps the movies have an eternal stranglehold on me as I either fall "in love" at first sight or not at all. Sylvia reminded me of a girl years back in 4-H Club who sang "Candy Kisses" in a slightly nasal though I thought beautiful voice. Beauty all around us.

Rosie poured some coffee and sat down heavily with her bacon and eggs. "Want some of this?" I shook my head no. She became conspiratorial. "If Tim doesn't marry Sylvia there's lots of guys around here that will. She got half a dozen proposals after a swimming party." Rosie laughed with a decidedly masculine bahaha effect, her breasts and neck quivering gelatinously. "Sylvia knit her bikini out of a *Cosmopolitan* pattern and you should have seen them eyes pop!" Sylvia blushed again. I began to feel uncomfortable. A slow fire stirred below. They used to call this configuration of emotions a "crush" and

I had in an hour begun to feel the weight of it. Blood moved into my face and Rosie's bacon made me nauseated.

"I'm going for a walk." I nearly tripped in my momentum to the door. I went out to the car and fished around for my toothbrush and pills. No Valium until the whiskey wears off, I reminded myself. I looked at the bottles of vitamins—B complex, E, 250-mg C—and they depressed me. Argh. Is nothing natural? On Tristan da Cunha they eat fish and are happy. Musk-ox milk and seal fat for the Aleuts. Swim with sea otters and learn their tricks. A compulsive about vitamins; if I went without them a week my body would vaporize into detached molecules of filth. Tim had said after his shower in my room, "Why do you take all those fucking vitamins?" I don't know. I lit a cigarette and watched a few cars pass, housewives off to the grocers while the dad sleeps in. Pleasant enough town. Maybe I could hide out here but who's looking for me. Get a job. Marry Sylvia. Go bass fishing weekends. I began to think of the bass-fishing equipment I would need. An open face Shakespeare Ambassador reel and a stout casting rod with a tackle box full of daredevils, pikie minnows, jitterbugs, mepps, spoons. And wire clip leaders.

Rosie came down the stairs in toreadors pushed to their limit, curlers in her hair wrapped with a scarf and large aqueous blue sunglasses. "Going shopping." She waved. I decided to go back up and sleep in her bed.

A few hours later when I awoke to Buck Owens singing "Together Again" I had no idea where I was. Then I remembered seeing Sylvia walk from the bathroom to the bedroom in her robe and falling to sleep to the bilious sound of my stomach in full recoil. And dreaming of standing on a coral outcropping beside a lagoon. There were large tailing permit, a splendid fish, but I had no equipment and I was frantic. I opened my eyes and watched Rosie unpack groceries and open another beer. I stood and stretched in my shorts.

"Put on some pants or I'll get horny." She brought me a beer and I sat on the edge of the couch sipping it. She put on a new Dolly Parton album she had bought at the grocery store. Parton has a clear, at times rather tremulous, soprano, but often shrieks and yells. She's frightening, the sort of woman one is attracted to but afraid of; too much of it there for this young neurotic dog. No frenzies please, just be peaceful and preferably demure. How much better Rosie carries her fat than that girl who wanted a ride to Miami. I thought I heard Tim call and I walked to the door. He called again and I opened it. He was sitting up in bed. Sylvia was asleep beside him, breathing deeply on the sheet, wearing only a pair of lollipop white panties. Tim rolled his eyes and I nodded my head approvingly and handed him the beer.

"I'm going to get a tape deck put in the car and we'll be out of here by midnight."

"How much do they cost?" I liked tapes in a car but thought them rather expensive.

"I know where I can charge it."

Then Sylvia turned in the bed and drew her legs up, still sleeping.

"She's a goddamn knockout, huh?" I felt like going back and getting on my trousers before my interest become apparent. But I sat down not wanting to miss anything. There was a photo on the dresser of Tim in an old Mercury stock car, a number 33 painted on the side. He looked very young and had a duck's-ass haircut. Rosie came in with two beers after turning the record player up. A nice breeze was lifting the curtains, bringing in the odor of a flower I didn't recognize. It was similar though to jasmine and from that moment onward I always thought of Sylvia in terms of that odor.

"If this is a gangbang I want to be in on it." Rosie sat down and looked at Tim with narrowed eyes.

"I'd lay you, Rosie, but I'm just too tired. Why don't you pick on him." I quickly looked up in the air. Then Sylvia awoke and tried to pull the sheet around her but Tim grabbed it back off. "You Baptists are so chickenshit." She smiled. Evidently it was a joke of some standing as she made no further move to cover herself.

5

FRANK came over just before dinner and he and Rosie necked for a few minutes, then she dismissed him to finish the cooking. He regarded me rather sullenly as if I were some sort of ardent competitor for the prize. I offered him a drink from a bottle of Wild Turkey I had bought an hour before and was suckling nervously on to destroy the notion that I was in the wrong place and the displacement might be fatal. Sylvia and Tim had been gone several hours to get the tape deck and the car tuned. Now Frank stared at me as he took the bottle and gulped, his adam's apple bobbing.

Frank looked like a criminal turkey, gaunt and sallow. In ages past he would have been described as "craven"; I had begun to think of many of the crackers as Englishmen, say from the eighteenth century, with generations of bad diet and the sort of line breeding that causes a genetic horror show in domestic animals. Southness. Somehow a warmer sort than the North owns but oddly more potentiality for meanness. All the chancre is open to the air with much of the imagination loosed from the prospect of making money thus more inventive and mischievous. In the North Frank would have kept busy in the

Buick plant in Flint and his income would be a small fortune in Harlan County, Kentucky.

Maybe the cold makes us more economically resourceful. I could remember while I was staring down the amber neck of the Turkey bottle all of those blue, glittery sub-zero dawns when I delivered the newspaper in a small town with the sidewalks too rutted with ice to use my bike and the cars with snow tires clanking and shaking with their chains. Businessmen would greet me through their mufflers and mackinaws. I showed promise. The papers got through and were always dry and cold, being placed in the milkboxes where on especially cold mornings the cream would congeal, freeze, pop up the bottle like a white turd. Then to use the bike and rip open a tire on a shard of ice would consume the profit from a month's labor in the repairs. The cold is plainly an imposition, a horrible thing. The breath is icy smoke, pants cuffs freeze, the schoolroom stinking with thawing wool. Even the scrotum tightens in its sack and retreats, the penis withdraws. The floated bored faces skating around and around, then singing carols and drinking cocoa with marshmallows not quite melting in the scum. There was a Christmas dinner when the furnace broke down and it was twenty below and the family and relatives toyed with their food all decrepitly bundled in the dining room, growing more desperate as the gravy solidified and their breath became visible. The barn fire that melted a circle, with the perimeter gray and foul—smoke still singeing the nose, and the cattle bloated and stiff-legged smelling sour of burned hair in an ashtray. The farmer and wife both red-eyed seeing their prize dairy herd cooked. Didn't even melt much snow and the fire pump truck's pitiful thousand gallons of water now frozen a foot thick everywhere so that the curious were slipping. Those very few, perhaps two or three doctors' wives, who could afford a short trip to Florida were thought vaguely decadent.

53

"You ever fish for cats?"

Frank was staring at me. For a moment I thought of dragging very wet cats out of the river then it occurred to me he was talking about catfish.

"No. They're too far south of us, south of Grand Rapids. The water's too cold where I live."

"I caught a channel cat last week that weighed thirty. Rosie get the picture."

Rosie went over and rummaged in a desk drawer. She handed me the photo leaving a grease splotch on the corner. Frank was standing holding the fish toward the camera to make it look even larger. Rosie was off to the side in an unattractive bathing suit with her huge sunglasses, holding a can of beer. I handed the photo to Frank and his face clouded.

"Rosie you got grease on the picture, you asshole."

"Fuck you and your fish," she said, back at the stove.

"It was real good eating. At Raiford the food was shit. I'll never go back to Florida again. Cleaning drain ditches. Snakes all over and the niggers wanting to stick a pick into your head."

I wanted to ask him about prison but Tim and Sylvia came through the door. Sylvia was in shorts and a halter and the white shorts were pulled very tightly across her buttocks. One thought of Georgia peaches or even Anjou pears. Tim began talking about the car and the tape deck. He carried a small suitcase of tapes which Rosie and Frank picked over.

"You're drinking again," Sylvia said to me, raising her eyebrows but smiling. Tim took the bottle and looked at the level and had several gulps. I had an unpleasant feeling in the wishbone, partly from Sylvia and partly I suspected from the half quart of whiskey. I began to think the misrepresentation was chemical. Sylvia doesn't know much: aside from magazines there is no reading material to speak of in the apartment. While I was dozing on the couch I could smell faintly the odor of kerosene. And began to think that the Depression was going on in the room behind me—Valdosta in 1933. What it is is a measureless and ignorant grace that owes nothing at all to girlishness. It is so easy to become fatigued with love. My mind held a picture of two rains: a light sprinkle when I stopped with a girl under a flowering quince near a brown muddy river at night and the moisture in the air lightly falling increased the odor of the quince and when it began to rain harder and we ran for my car a hundred or so yards away we smelled like quince in the confines of the car with the steaming windshield, the metallic rattling of the rain on the hood. The other took place on Fifty-seventh Street in New York on a hot August afternoon walking out of a matinee with a girl I knew I was going to break from that evening. The rain was warm and the streets had that hot cement smell and we stood under the marquee simply watching it fall wordlessly. Sylvia was the equal of those two standing in the rain I thought and hoped she would betray some unpardonable vulgarity very soon so that I would not have to think about her.

And Tim, all that conscienceless vigor would soon fail him, as it does most between the mid- and late twenties or early thirties when one first realizes one is alive and that like all other living creatures one has a beginning, a middle and a terribly certain end.

And because of our rather mindless and disorganized plot there is a stiffness in the room. Even Frank seems to sense it. The eve of battle. They went forth. I had a rather yellow sense in my belly that the whole project was ten degrees off in the direction of the wacky. And began to hope that the project would metamorphose into an aimless joyride, a sightseeing tour with perhaps some good fishing thrown in. Tim and Sylvia could either watch or screw up on the bank or back in the bushes. And watching the others now through the sweet blur of whiskey I began to realize just how tentative my interest in life itself was—I did not qualify even as an observer let alone a pilgrim. Or to make it tiresome, I was not in the stands watching or on the field playing, I was down in some sub-basement regarding the whole base structure indifferently. My friends no longer existed, neither did my wife; I had no state or country, no governor or president. We used to call such people nihilists but that is much too strong a word for a vacuum. But the juice still seemed to be there, no matter how narrowed and atrophied. The delight in the air and water and trees and in such rare creatures as Sylvia, and the food that even now Rosie was slinging on the table. And in whiskey. And fishing. The brain seems to make its own little governments. The project was only a novelty, some sort of Coronation Ball.

When we finally sat down to supper I felt that I was in the hands of foreigners, possibly enemies. I wanted to remember a time when I could walk up a wall backwards, a mythic seizure in the past when reality was successfully flouted as it never really is. It all seemed so helplessly accidental; a day and a half before I was in the middle of my usual excitement over fishing and now I was within hours of leaving for the West, the ostensible reason being to blow up a dam.

But then we all began to eat aggressively, an essentially homely function that most of the time quiets any fluttering brain. There were smoked pork hocks, fresh spinach, new potatoes with gravy and biscuits. Those simple country-girl types actually knew how to cook. None of the brown rice and raw vegetable horseshit. We ate in almost total silence listening to Marty Robbins sing "Devil Woman," a monumentally absurd song.

Sylvia tried to help Rosie with the dishes but Rosie said we should get on our way. I looked at Sylvia's cheap suitcase and thought of all the Southern girls that I had seen standing rather forlornly in bus stations in Cincinnati or Atlanta, a kind of tawdry prettiness about them compared to girls in New York

City or California. And they tended to smile a lot as if they were born to please. I walked out to the car and got in the back seat while they were saying their farewells that I had no part in. My own wife had driven me to the airport in addition to loaning me the fare, an emotionless process that followed months of talk where no one was really wrong because no one had ever been right.

Barely light. And a dark green against the window, a wall of green with my eye a few inches from it. Tim and Sylvia were breathing heavily with sleep in front of me, with a few strands of her hair over the head rest. Mosquitoes and sour air with all the windows up. The car was parked tight to the foliage on a very narrow country lane. How did we get here? Through the windshield I could see down a long isle of green split by the sandy trail that disappeared into ground fog. But something was moving and my skin prickled. The shape came closer and seemed to be floating in the fog moving toward the car. It was a black man carrying his lunch pail. Then our horn beeped and the man jumped then shrugged and passed the car with his eyes averted. The birds were silent.

"Timmy?" Sylvia said.

Tim yawned and stretched. "I didn't see him until he was right in front of us so I beeped."

We were somewhere off Route 90 near Cuevas on the other side of Gulfport. The night before I had told Tim that I thought we could buy dynamite around Bisbee or Douglas in Arizona. There's a lot of mining in that area. I had gotten a bit out of hand in the first few hundred miles what with finishing the whiskey and starting on another bottle. But all I really had done was go through the old false life story routine and then Tim and I had exchanged sexual anecdotes after which Sylvia had interjected that we were "sick" and that had started a long argument.

Now I felt rather sorry about my unremitting foulness of the
night before. It certainly had gotten the Sylvia question out of
the way, or seemed to at least. When we had stopped for coffee
her eyes were red from crying. Tim laughed and I pretended
disinterest. The mood is a strange one. I mean this wanting to
slaughter some lovely feeling in your brain—of course the psy-
chology of it is open and only of nominal interest. Thank Christ
people have almost stopped talking about such things.

At the diner when Sylvia went into the washroom Tim
started laughing again. "She's faking. She can fuck my ears
off."

I thought about it when she walked back to the table with
every trucker in the place staring at her then at us with some
hostility. Who's getting the goodies, they probably wondered.
Not me. Probably never. I was surprised when she didn't seem
angry.

"I'm sorry," I said.

"No you're not." She was smiling, if vaguely.

Tim laughed. "You can't fool this sweet little bitch." She
punched him lightly in the shoulder, her smile broadening.
"Why some of the things she likes just about make me blush."
Now she blushed and stared at her food.

Tim revved the engine and drove up the trail looking for a
place to turn around. We came to a small shack with a bare
yard and backed in. I could see faces in the window, probably
the home of the man Tim frightened.

"You shouldn't have beeped," I said.

"I know. I get jumpy when I wake up."

I leaned over the seat and we began talking about routes.
Sylvia had fallen back to sleep in the bucket seat and it was
difficult not to stare at her legs which seemed so glaringly bare
and beautiful.

"They're the best I've ever seen," Tim said.

"Yes." She moved sideways a little in the seat and her panties were clearly visible and the trace of a soft mound which was darker underneath the whiteness of the panties. I slumped back on the seat feeling like a shabby voyeur. There was a lump in my throat and my temples pounded with my hangover. I wanted to be in love momentarily. Maybe the inaccessibility of her made me desire her so much.

We pulled into a small restaurant near the entrance to Route 90. "Sylvia, wake up." He shook her with roughness. "He's been staring at your cunt for hours." She was wide awake and glanced at me angrily when she pulled her skirt down.

"That's a goddamn lie."

Tim shrieked and skipped into the restaurant. Sylvia brushed her hair back and got out. She shivered and tucked her blouse neatly into her skirt.

"Sylvia, that's a lie. I mean what Tim said." She only took my arm and we walked into the restaurant where Tim was already bullshitting the waitress.

"See those two," he said to the waitress. "They're on their honeymoon. They sure look tired. I bet they're sex maniacs."

The waitress giggled and stared at Sylvia. I quickly went to the men's room and looked at my swollen face. Perhaps it wasn't me. That was the displacement problem. How could I be sure. For once it didn't seem to matter much. I was along for the ride. Maybe we would do something interesting. If we blew up some dam it would have a sort of final interest to it like a fishing record that couldn't be taken away from you.

PART II

CHAPTER

FROM the balcony you could see the tops of buildings covered
with tar and stones and then the dry riverbed of the White-
water and beyond the riverbed Agua Prieta. On a hill to the
right outside of Agua Prieta are a dozen white adobe buildings
forming a square, the cantinas and whorehouses. At dawn and
for a few hours afterwards the sky is very blue but before mid-
morning the heat changes this and the sky becomes a sort of
dull silver and the heat rises to a hundred degrees. When the
breeze is just right you get a continuous stream of the fouled
air from the huge copper smelter outside of Douglas. Douglas
is a town of more than average ugliness but it makes up for its
ugliness by its contiguity to Mexico, and even more by its air
of the faded but still active cowtown, and the fact that it sits
on land once fought over by the United States Cavalry and the
fabled Mescalero Apache and also the Chiricahua. The White-
water River is a joke as no river in southern Arizona is merely
allowed to flow; the water is diverted to feed something
whether it is cotton or cattle.

In the room behind the balcony the large wood-paddled fan

drifts concentrically with insufficient power to make any difference. Below the fan the room is bright and hot and not very well appointed. There are two large double beds and a few chairs and lamps and a dull green carpet. The bathroom is as big, though, as any bathroom in the Plaza Hotel in New York. You are tempted to close the door and sit there with the shower running cold which provides an amateurish but efficient imitation of air-conditioning.

It was nearly noon when I awoke and after watching the fan for a few moments and going through a short countdown to make sure of my location I got up to go to the bathroom. Tim wasn't in the other bed but Sylvia was, quite nude, with the sheet straggling off onto the floor. She was on her side facing me so that when I walked to the bathroom I glanced at her rear. I stood there for a moment looking at it then out the window at the hotel parking lot. The car was still there. She moved a little on the bed and I took three steps further toward the bathroom. I frankly didn't want to be caught in so awkward a position. I merely stood there tasting the irony of the picture: nude man who loves nude woman sprawled on the bed but they have never touched nor does it seem very likely. In the shower I doubted that I had fully memorized her body and wanted to take another look. I took a grand assortment of vitamins but doubted they would outweigh the chili rellenos and tequila of the night before.

Where was Tim? We had gotten in town the evening before then crossed the bridge into Agua Prieta. Events became less well defined after that. I remembered walking back with Sylvia. I remembered chewing on a single peyote cactus and thinking better of it. That was why my mouth tasted as if I had been eating oak leaves. Then there was the bar at the whorehouse and a scene of sorts.

When I got out of the bathroom Sylvia's eyes were open and she had drawn the sheet up.

"Where's Timmy?"

"I don't know."

"I guess I want to go home."

I said nothing. I found my Levi's and drew them on facing away from her. Then I slid them off deciding to go back to bed. I felt a bit nauseated and wanted to wait for the world to steady itself.

"There's no point in going home. This has to be at least more interesting than Valdosta."

"I don't think so. You and Timmy are getting so crazy and I'm not sitting another night in that whorehouse. I thought we were going to the Grand Canyon. I go along with things because Timmy's screwed up but this is no good. Maybe he's still over there. Shut your eyes. I'm getting up."

"It's too late," I said. "You had nothing on when I got up."

"Shut your eyes anyway."

Sylvia got out of bed and walked to the bathroom. I watched and she turned and looked at me from the door. "You're an asshole," she said. That was the first time she used such a word.

I woke up again an hour later and the room was empty. I had a painful hard-on. We had gone a bit too far I thought. After an insane amount of travel fatigue we got into Douglas and without eating had gone over to Agua Prieta and had a half dozen margaritas apiece except Sylvia who had maybe three and then ate dinner. By then it was close to midnight and we were all hyped up. Tim dropped a few pills and then we let a Mexican guide us to a whorehouse without telling Sylvia where we were going. There was a mariachi band in the cantina that fronted rather feebly for the whorehouse and I danced several times with Sylvia who seemed very happy. Then Tim flipped a coin and I went into the back first but settled on a blow job as the girl didn't seem too attractive. When I got back Tim had told Sylvia what was going on. I thought she was going to cry. Then Tim disappeared with a bar girl who kept shrieking *"arriba, arriba"* to the music. Sylvia was very pale and I tried to cheer her up.

"How could you go with her? She's not even pretty."

"Tim's got you and I don't have anybody here," I answered rather lamely.

"Then why did he go with that girl?"

I shrugged, wondering myself. I had a brief vision of repeating the act with Sylvia which made me shudder. We waited for an hour for Tim then Sylvia asked me to walk her home because she didn't feel safe by herself and she was leaving. I told the bartender who spoke English to give the message to Tim. When we got back to the hotel there was an edge of dawn and I went immediately to bed. When Sylvia got out of the bathroom I could see her get into bed in the lessening darkness.

"I love you," I said.

"That's liquor talking."

"No it's not." Then I went to sleep.

Now I wondered if I should go look for Tim but dismissed the notion because it was very hot and I was sweating just lying there. My nausea though had passed and I felt hungry. There was a half-empty tequila bottle on the nightstand and I took a slug, feeling the warm liquid sear its way to my stomach. I heard a key in the lock and decided to feign sleep. There were a few flies buzzing around my face and through a squinted eye I could see that it was Sylvia and that she had brought me some coffee. Good girl. Now marry me. I heard the springs of her bed. She must be sitting wondering where Tim is. I must breathe more deeply and I'm sure she must think me absurd and embarrassing with my hard-on pointed up under the sheet. Maybe not. I've never known women very well and deeply and she might not be thinking any such thing or she might be thinking that it might be nice to sit on it for a moment as I know she and Tim haven't been together for three days. All that speed and alcohol too. Of course I would want to stay awake if someone were shooting at me I think. And Demerol's a sweet world in a way. I opened one eye slightly but she was looking at me.

"What time is it?" I asked.

"About two. You should eat something or you'll get a head-ache."

I turned on my side and drank the coffee. She was looking rather blankly over my body and out the window over the small balcony.

"You can see that whorehouse from here," she said.

"Yeah. I wish I was over there. It cures a hangover."

"Are they fun?"

She acted interested in knowing and I mulled over a number of answers. None seemed quite right.

"Not really fun. Except the most expensive ones in places like New York or Boston or London. Then it's just about like any girl only more skillful. Last night it was like buying something from a store. Not too much fun."

"A man in Atlanta once when Rosie and I went up there overnight shopping offered me fifty dollars."

"What did you do?"

"I started laughing and he got angry and walked away. We were in a bar. Rosie is always glad to do it for free."

"And you aren't?"

"No. I've only made love to Timmy and to another guy last year when I got drunk. Timmy screws everyone he wants. He doesn't want to get married."

"Don't tell him what I told you last night."

She paused, obviously not remembering. I was disappointed. It was apparent that I was not being taken seriously.

"You were only drunk. You don't love me. You only want to screw me and I should probably let you. It doesn't make any difference."

67

"It makes a lot a of difference to me. Nobody wants a sympathy fuck. I would never fuck a girl again if it was a sympathy fuck."

I had gotten instantly angry. Anything that borders on mothering or sympathy has always made me angry. She shrugged and walked over to the bathroom. I could hear the shower running and instantly regretted my big mouth when I thought of her in the shower.

The open window served as a hot air vent and I began to fantasize about glaciers and snow and the trips I had made into the mountains when the temperature never rose much above forty-five and was well below freezing in the middle of the night. When you got up at dawn say in the shadow of a mountain wall there was always a rime of frost on your sleeping bag. I always looked out from this dark clear light at the sun shining on some meadow or mammoth rock formation or small lake whose surface was invariably dimpled with trout rising. In the fifteen hundred or so miles we had driven I didn't see one likely trout stream or river. All the water looked sluggish and brown and warm. And I only drove perhaps two hundred of the miles. Tim was too flighty and nervous when anyone else was driving, especially Sylvia who had made a miscalculation while passing another car near Houston and had nearly finished us all. When I did drive I admittedly was too taken with Sylvia's chatter and her long legs, something that Tim picked up on right away even while trying to doze. But he did not seem to take such threats seriously, in fact, didn't seem to take my immediate affection for Sylvia as a threat at all. I found out why near New Iberia in Louisiana where after a big meal of crawfish and beer I crawled into the back seat and began snoring but then became half awake with general discomfort. I heard them talking rather low and steadily, first about why Tim hadn't returned to her after he got out of the hospital. He had gone to Los Angeles with a hospital

friend and stayed wrecked for a month, then got in trouble in
a fight and the judge let him go to Key West rather than jail.
After all he had served two hitches or tried to serve two
hitches. But he had no notion of settling down anywhere much
less in Valdosta. And he said if he ever married anyone it
would be Sylvia but he knew he wouldn't get married. He
didn't want to be a mechanic in a Ford garage like his older
brother or a gas jockey like his younger and he knew it was too
late for him to go back to Georgia Tech. Sylvia had evidently
been pregnant but miscarried and I could tell that she had
counted on this at one time for drawing him back. But then
his speech became more excitable, dreamier, like so many
speed rips one hears. He either wanted to go to Alaska and
work on the pipeline they were going to build or maybe go to
Africa to be a professional soldier. He had known two ser-
geants who went to Angola to fight in a private army. The
money was supposed to be great. No, he hadn't heard from
them. Such people don't write letters. She was silent for a long
time, terribly depressed I figured. So many good women fall
in love with maniacs I thought. Then Tim held up the slight
hope for her that he might go to Australia and if he liked it and
got a job he cared for he might send for her.

It was all very pitiful in a way. These two didn't seem to be-
long to the twentieth century though they bore so many of its
characteristic scars. I've always wondered how people who
don't know anything about history get by but I've realized if
you are ignorant of history you're not lost in it. Sylvia was only
intent, it seemed, on some age-old mating procedure and felt
a certain desperation in having given over six or seven years to
a man whose conception of a proper life must have come from
an old Errol Flynn movie. So simple and almost charming if
you didn't know and care for them, a particularly foolish country song set into action. And she would out of an almost bio-
logical drive probably return home and marry finally someone

she didn't love at all but have children she did love. She did
not entertain alternatives.

As we crossed Texas which seemed the width of earth itself
even at a steady ninety miles an hour the misery started to
spread. Australia passed with the scenery, was discarded for
Alaska again or maybe becoming a hunting guide in British
Columbia. When I was awake and not too drunk or comatose
with depression we talked about hunting and fishing and in a
very childish manner about women. Absurd things like the
total justification of the double standard. You would naturally
kill someone if they screwed your wife. That was assumed. But
they were only attitudes for me that were believed because one
repeated them, like the lies one repeated until they owned
their own inalterable reality. I had decided to visit my wife
four months before but stopped three blocks away and settled
on glassing the house for intruders. I saw her put my daughter
in the car and drive to the grocery store after wiping the snow
from the windshield. An hour later I saw her come back from
the grocery store with two bags of groceries and my daughter.
I saw my dog trot down the far side of the street sniffing and
pissing on an occasional lamppost. That evening I got quite
drunk and called her saying I was in Philadelphia of all places
and I might find a job that would draw the whole thing out of
the fire. But then there was little fire left except the anti-
mechanics of inertia; those married tend to stay married until
. . . And as I became less sure of myself she gathered
strength, became more shrewd and protective, and I began to
find the clarity of her intelligence offensive. It seemed that over
ten thousand dollars' worth of Wellesley had prepared her for
someone other than me.

The shower had stopped but Sylvia hadn't come out. It occurred to me that she didn't think herself beautiful. She was
beautiful in the way a model is beautiful and outside a few

big cities the conception of beauty is a certain well-stacked perky cuteness, something I've always loathed. Sylvia was slender but many men I know would have thought her too skinny.

I got up finally and dressed to go eat. It must be nearing three o'clock. I wondered idly where Tim was and looked out the window to see the Dodge there glittering in the heat with so many thousands of dollars' worth of other cars. There was even a Winnebago Camper, the sort that costs at least twelve grand and retired couples drive them aimlessly throughout the country collecting stickers and curios. Sylvia came out of the bathroom in bra and panties brushing her damp hair. I was startled.

"I guess there's no point in being real formal," she said. She leaned over to get a blouse from her suitcase and her panties were semi-transparent. I felt vaguely ill.

"No, there's no point being formal. I had three sisters who walked around bare-ass all the time."

We both turned, hearing the key in the door. It was Tim and he looked very bad as if suffering from terminal exhaustion. Sylvia walked over and kissed him. "We were worried about you."

He laughed and said over her shoulder that we must have fucked our brains out. Sylvia started crying and went back in the bathroom and locked the door. He beat at the door and said he was only kidding.

"Well, while you were fucking around I bought two cases of dynamite plus the caps. We have to drive up to Bisbee this afternoon to get them. Or tomorrow morning."

CHAPTER

7

THESE gestures of importance! Tito pauses on the edge of the small spring. He is acting reverential, holding his straw hat in his hands and against his chest. A postcard Chicano now playing to the three of us. Sylvia is plainly touched. Tim is plainly bored. We have walked three miles from the trail end and it has been incredibly hot—I watched a sweat spot on the back of Sylvia's blouse grow to the size of a crow. Sweat trickled down my legs. Tim walked directly behind Tito who led the way. I don't think Tim slept more than an hour again last night. Tito is selling us the two cases of dynamite and caps at I think twice the normal price but we must first look at his favorite place in the mountains, a place he visited often in his youth both to bathe and for its beauty. I admit there is not a beer can in sight and it is above the elevation where one usually finds rattlesnakes. On the way up we saw a roadrunner and a small offshoot of an arroyo where some javelinas made their home, a foul-smelling cul-de-sac in the mesquite. My nose is so sweaty the sunglasses slide on the ridge. The point is that we had to look at Tito's shrine before he gyps us on the dynamite. A strenuous irony here. How can air be thin and still hot. We have found out unfortunately that anyone in Arizona can go into a hardware store and buy dynamite. So for extra money we are getting a large dose of exhaustion.

"It is very beautiful?" Tito says.

"Yes," Sylvia murmurs. Tim and I nod assent. You can see deeply into the spring where some minnows are darting about and I am a bit stunned that there are minnows way up here. We all sit down on the rock with wary eyes for any creatures. There are many animal prints in the sand along the water's edge.

"Is it good to drink?" I ask. Tito gives me a falsely energetic si si si and we both crouch and drink. Cold enough to make the teeth ache. I stand and shed my clothes and Tim follows suit. Tito pauses with a deviously shy look at Sylvia then strips. We all jump in the water which is gloriously cold.

"If you don't come in I'll throw you in," Tim shouts at Sylvia. The shout rolls down the small canyon and is lost far below us. Sylvia takes her clothes off except her bra and panties and steps into the shallow water. Tim signals me with a nod of his head and I move toward her right feeling like a foolish alligator. Tim slides up and grabs her ankles. She is laughing and even continues laughing when she catches what he has in mind. He holds her around the waist tightly while I undo her bra which doesn't fall. Then I slip her panties down her legs and she lifts each foot so they won't get wet. I can see Tito staring rather wide-eyed out in the pool with only his Indian head and shiny black hair above the water. We splash around for a half hour then sit back on the warm rocks drying out.

The water was as clear as Bimini and when I sank beneath it I could see Sylvia's body very clearly but was reminded unpleasantly of all those underwater nude photos I saw through my youth in *Playboy* and how if you lived way up in the uneventfully Protestant woods the pictures caused a terrible sort of groin disease. Beautiful girls playing naked in the sunny water while the fifteen-year-old student athlete looks out at the snow-banks. He is doing poorly in geometry even though the theorems are printed in red. The magazine has been passed to him along the row of desks. It is a hot country of bodies and he feels his member rising under the desk. His girl friend who sits across the aisle stares at him disapprovingly. She is Methodist and there is small chance that she will ever frolic bare-ass in the sun. He feels cheated that he is not elsewhere.

Tim lights a large joint he has drawn from his shirt pocket and we pass it back and forth and for a change Sylvia takes a very deep drag.

"A margarita would be a lot better." I am thirsty for something tangier than the spring water.

"I want a can of beer and a hotdog," Tim says. Then he notices that poor Tito who is sitting on the other side of Sylvia is gazing at her and has become erect. "Watch out Sylvia. He's going to rape you." She glances at Tito and blushes. Tito jumps up and pulls on his trousers and wanders off to the other side of the pool. He pretends to be examining the plant life. Sylvia begins giggling.

"Mexicans like light-haired women," I announce sententiously. Tito looks across at me with no little hatred. He reminds me of my dog who on emerging from our apartment would grab a stick or a jump rope or ball and stand very arrogantly looking off in the distance. Sylvia is leaning forward staring at her toes and Tim pushes his hand under her butt and twitches his fingers. She jumps up and swings at him and he quickly pushes her backward into the water.

"You bastard. I didn't want to get my hair wet." Sylvia clears her hair out of her eyes standing mid-thigh deep in the water. Behind her Tito is standing in the shadow of a rock ledge. For a moment the scene is frozen before me like the frame in a movie is frozen in that contemporary vogue: Sylvia lifting back her hair, her shoulders and stomach and thighs covered with

74

droplets against which the sun glints so that the droplets are turned reflectory. And the clear blue water and the deflection of her legs beneath the skin of water—the figure in the shadows behind her so resolutely ludicrous. I felt a momentary pity for myself because the scene couldn't be withdrawn. It was now a permanent hole in my memory and I figured that in twenty years I would be able to recall the vision though it would be flat and still as a painting. And some of the color would naturally fade and the sharp planes of light and shadow would disappear, even the slight shadow between her upper thigh and cleft as she turned away from the sun, smoothly using her middle to turn with instead of her shoulders. There was even a brief sense of freedom, a clear but torturous happiness. While she stood there letting the sun dry her again we dressed and chattered about what we wanted to eat and drink. Then we watched Sylvia dress and Tim decided we should drive up to Tucson when we reached the car.

We walked back down the arroyo slowly. Sylvia was developing a blister behind her sandal strap so Tito tore his handkerchief in half and wrapped it around the strap. I was mildly stoned and my legs jolted unpleasantly in their sockets with each downward step.

The second night in Douglas and Agua Prieta had been better than the first though there were moments that couldn't be described as anything but horrifying. We had covered all the cantinas in the square, dawdling for at least two hours in one that specialized in transvestites, actually false transvestites as they were only homosexuals dressed and rather prettily as young women. Sylvia was very startled when she learned they weren't female though she sensed something was wrong. Everyone stared rather cattily at her which made her uncomfortable. One of the "girls" sat with us and had a drink. She ran her hand up and down Tim's leg until it seemed he was on the verge of giving her a tumble. She began nuzzling his ear and

then kissed him and Sylvia got up to walk out on the mess. I
followed her out and we stood under the marquee of the bar
looking vacantly at the lights of the dozen cantinas with their
discordant mariachi bands and jukeboxes blending almost har-
monically. The night was very warm and smelled unpleasant.
I tried to explain to her that it was inconceivable that Tim
would hurt her on purpose. He acted on impulse and liked to
have fun though the fun might strike her as a bit strange at
times. I had begun to feel a bit guilty: without me we wouldn't
have been in a whorehouse or in Agua Prieta or on our clearly
absurd mission to blow up a dam which Tim merely adopted
again on impulse. I was the frayed and immoderately ugly
brains of the project. Maybe Tim would have grown tired of
speed and wandering around and returned to her. What we
were doing didn't help. He was happy, maniacally happy, and
you could see he didn't want it to end. While we were talking
I understood why I cared so much for her, at least in part: she
was an antique, reminding me of the comparatively simple
country girls I had gone to high school with a decade before.
And she was helplessly feminine. We were breaking her in
pieces yet she moved with us as if she either had no character
or simply wanted to please. What else could she do? I kissed
her cheek lightly with my hand around her waist. Her eyes
were moist and I told her she shouldn't cry again as that only
made the whole thing worse than it was. A group of locals
were watching so we went back into the bar. Tim was sitting
alone and got up to meet us.

"Let's get the fuck out of here. She had bad breath. I can't
stand bad breath."

It became good for a few hours then. We had a fine dinner
of Guaymas shrimp with a lot of wine then walked around
arm in arm laughing. We played pool for an hour and I won
thirty bucks off Tim but he refused to pay me unless I spent it
on a girl of his choice. I said he would choose a hog. Sylvia

was mildly drunk and tried to make Tim promise he wouldn't
go with a girl but stay with her as she was much better than
they were. I felt sorry for her then as Tim always accepted an
admonition as a challenge to do otherwise. He teased her that
she was turning into a whore too and said he liked her better
that way. She seemed pleased and asked him to take her back
to the hotel which he refused to do. I only stared down into
my double shot of tequila. These little scenes were exhausting;
she apparently saw him as he must have been years before, less
intractable and without any Methadrine or fatalism in his
blood, though when she became frantic it seemed to me that
she was beginning to understand that it was hopeless.

And there was no sense of balance left in anything we were
doing. All that had begun as an innocent boozy comment crossing Duval Street so many miles away had become fact and we
weren't accomplishing anything but pulling our own particular
emotional plugs. Like so much reality it was merely what we
were not "not" doing—I mean walking home that night and
standing on the bridge dividing the countries looking down in
the dark sandy dry riverbed. I was tired of imagining actions
and having them come down to merely nothing, or something
as confused as what we were taking part in. It was all as mud-
dled as turning to my left and seeing United States and turning
right to see Mexico. I needed a few days of fishing to sort my
feelings out or better yet to lose all my feelings. And who were
these two strangers with me and why had we caused ourselves
to be where we were.

I took my pool-game payment out on a very pleasant older
woman and when I came back to the table and said that she
was fantastic, which she was, Tim had to try her too. If I had
kept my mouth shut I could have made Sylvia momentarily
happy. But in the ensuing quarrel he told her that she was becoming a pain in the ass and he would put her on the bus the
next day. So we walked back in silence with Tim refusing my

urgings to have them go ahead and make peace. He only said that there was nothing to settle. It was a very dull drunkenness I felt, so that in the room when we took turns at the bathroom I felt nothing when I saw Sylvia partially nude. I wanted a total blackout. I took the last shower and made it a long one hoping that Tim might make love to her which he hadn't done on the trip. But when I got out the room was dark and he was sitting on the edge of the bed sipping from the tequila bottle.

Somehow the next morning we awoke rather happily. During the night Sylvia had talked Tim out of sending her home. We all seemed to feel a sort of childish renewal out of driving up to Bisbee to get the dynamite. We would at least see the Grand Canyon by the next afternoon even though we agreed to start on smaller demolition projects and work our way up. At breakfast we even giggled over our pretentiousness; we had pored over the *Blaster's Handbook* and it became obvious that it was all much more complicated than we thought. The only bad feeling was caused by Tim having bought a pistol that first night in Mexico. I disliked pistols and thought that having one would mean a lot of trouble if we were ever stopped and searched. But Tim said that a pistol would be no harder to explain than the two cases of dynamite in the trunk.

Now walking down the arroyo on the steep path from the spring it seemed we were still happy. The late afternoon sun was becoming less hot and was casting clean dark shadows in the Pedregosas which were so dry-looking compared to the mountains I knew in Montana and Idaho. They reminded me of Ecuador and how unhappy I was spending a week in bed with dysentery and looking out at brown mountains that offered up no fantasies of fishing. We rode to Tito's in silence though Tito seemed quite happy at Tim's usual driving exhibition: we would go into mild four-wheel drifts on the corners, fishtail in second and move up to nearly a hundred on the

straightaway. Though I had confidence in Tim's driving when
he hadn't dropped too many pills I hated speed, even hated the
idea of motors, which I regarded as hostile. But I supposed
that Tim's best moments had been in driving stock cars back
in Georgia on those small dirt tracks in the pines at night with
not very good lighting and the cars and spectators being covered with red dust as the cars roared around in a tight circle in
second gear.

We reached a small settlement and Tito directed Tim into a
large yard where half a dozen children were playing softball.
There was a rather dingy stucco house placed in a cottonwood
grove with a shed in back among some junked cars. We loaded
the two cases from the shed into the trunk, gave Tito the
money and then Tito went inside and brought out four beers.
We sat and drank them in silence and then Tim began playing
softball with the children. He batted them grounders and then
a few fly balls. They asked him to hit a long one so he twirled
the ball, which was old and covered with black friction tape,
in his left hand, tossed it up and hit it very hard. We watched
it sail very high across the road into the mesquite. The children
clapped and shrieked. We sat and drank another beer and
Tito's wife came out and sat with us though she was very
plump and shy and said nothing. It was so peaceful that I was
disturbed when Tim said it was time to go. I could see that
Sylvia felt the same way, that Tito's yard was some sort of retreat for our exhausted bodies and nerves. We all shook hands
and when we got into the car Tito gave us a large joint, a true
bomber, which he said would make our trip to Tucson a good
one.

Tito's grass proved to be very good indeed—within moments
we were stoned. I thought it was the best I had ever had and
began thinking of trying to rid myself of my dependence on
alcohol which I thought, probably accurately, was slowly
wrecking my body. We stopped and ate at a Mexican restau-

rant where I had tripe stew or menudo while Tim and Sylvia ate hamburgers and watched me with distaste. Finally Tim ordered a bowl and ate it on my dare. He said that it tasted like last night's whore to which Sylvia made no comment.

We reached Tucson by nine at night and generally decided to try not to get too drunk or wrecked so we could get an early start for the Grand Canyon in the morning. We thought we would catch a movie and be in bed by midnight. On the way down Speedway on the south side of the city we passed a cinema that advertised a SUPER X EXTRA ADULT double feature. We quickly checked into a motel and drove back to the movie. Sylvia was mildly curious because she had never seen a skin flick before. The first feature was called *Greta* and proved to be a bit of a shock. A virginal girl (we guessed her to be about twenty-five) argues with her parents, leaves home and immediately falls into the hands of a gang of lesbians who work her over with vibrators and dildos until she becomes a convert. I was rather surprised as the girls were pretty and didn't resemble the women one used to see in the old American Legion hall black and white movies. Sylvia peeked out behind her fingers and gasped as if she were watching a horror show. The second feature involved a love-technique clinic and a mad doctor who attached willing women to a monstrously ingenious machine. We were fascinated.

SOMEONE once said and I think it was a Russian poet that we
are only the shadows of our imagination on earth. I sort of
liked the idea that the three of us were darting to and fro like
the minnows in the spring up in the Pedregosas while my poor
brain was somewhere else trying to create a superstructure for
what was taking place. Sylvia and Tim were "real people" and
thus didn't need a fresh metaphysic every day to be taken after
breakfast in one swallow. This seemed to increase my responsibility unpleasantly. I didn't want to lead. Perhaps within three
or four hours I could talk Tim into driving to Alaska or back to
Valdosta, then spend a week in Valdosta convincing him that
he should marry Sylvia. But maybe not. He had become ob-
sessed with the romantic aspects of sabotage and was always
fishing around in the *Blaster's Handbook* for useful information while Sylvia tended to dwell only on her love problems
and had forgotten, in fact, why we had come west in the first
place.

I was walking around the streets of Tucson after midnight.
When the movie let out I had told them I wanted to take a
walk and have a nightcap or two. Tim winked which was

mildly disgusting and Sylvia's eyes were fixed on something across the street. Sexuality. You watch other people.fucking and carrying on in Technicolor for a couple of hours and you get the startling idea that you might like to try it yourself. Or not. I felt "not." I was glutted with the aesthetic brutishness of those huge pumping organs and wished that I hadn't insisted that we sit in the front row. Tim had leaned forward with his elbows on his knees occasionally murmuring "Mother dog!" and "Jesus frog!" It was much too real in obvious comparison with reality itself. And after an hour it may as well have been stone gargoyles fucking. If I were to make such a movie I would proceed with infinite delicacy so that my hero, stunted with my own neuroticisms, would end up making love to a succession of slender international beauties in odd places: under a lilac bush, beside a meadow stream in Killarney, in a canopied bed, in a tent in Tanzania and so on. There would be no improperly sized dildos or battery operated instruments. Good grammar would be used. In the outdoor scenes birds would sing and a trout might rise in the stream and the woman would be on strict orders not to scream like a fishwife or stuck hog.

But then if the movies caused Tim to make love to Sylvia I guessed that they had served a purpose. And perhaps I was at fault for specializing my tastes. How often I had wanted to be Bob Bold and swagger around our great land having at every attractive girl, throwing in a homely waitress or two, even a grandmother out of kindness. It was never to be. Sadly, I never had trouble with whores but I knew that was because the act was so totally devoid of any response except the sexual. Like dogs. A very rare girl, Sylvia for instance, would throw me into a frenzy of trepidation: hollow stomach, trembling of hands, dry mouth and all of that. I had a brief vision of her and Tim together with her knees high against his back. I became angry and walked faster.

It took several doubles and a half hour of the Johnny Carson show in a bar called the Green Door to regain a semblance of calm. How much easier the whole trip would have been had Sylvia been less interesting. Much less, though. If she had been a cute dope I might have flown back to Key West by now, perhaps wangled a cheap trip to Bimini to bonefish. I would get some fishing in within a day or two on the way north. I asked the bartender if he had any maps but he was very busy and decided that I was either drunk or loony.

I more or less had our first dam picked out. It would be up in Idaho on a small branch of the Clearwater. There was another possibility near Ennis in Montana but the site was a little less secluded than the dam in Idaho where a wealthy rancher had ruined a good steelhead stream. The earthen dam he had constructed prevented steelhead from moving upstream to spawn while the dam near Ennis prevented brown trout from having the kind of water they like to spawn in. Both built out of greed and in contempt of the natural world.

I suddenly felt strong and clean and very moral. Slightly heroic, in fact. I turned on the barstool and looked at the roomful of collegiate hippie types, the counterculture on a liberal allowance. Some of the girls were admittedly interesting but I dismissed the idea of them because they vitiated my newly acquired heroic glow and also I didn't want to be reminded of Sylvia. The bartender advertised last call and I ordered a triple Granddad as a suitable sleeping pill. Narcosis with the liver hit by a club. The idea of sex movies and liquor depressed me. I grew up with the notion I might be a Jimmy Stewart type working a ranch in a valley with a fine trout stream running through it, a grand herd of Hereford cattle, and a lovely woman named Ramona or something like that as a helpmate. No time here for alcoholism or pornographic movies. The fantasy became errant—the closest movie had been fifty miles away and it featured year around Donald Duck and Francis the Talking

Mule movies. Would I expose Ramona to all that vulgar quacking? Ramona herself began quacking so I left the bar.

Out on the street I was unsure about the direction of the motel and cared less. Maybe a taxi to the airport was in order. But my fly rod and my pills. And Sylvia. What did I think I would do with her if I ever got her? The liquor seemed to swish in my guts as I searched for landmarks. I must have found the bar in a trance. Nothing was in the least familiar so I stopped a strolling couple and asked directions. She was so pretty that I didn't listen attentively and I was as lost as ever. O God get me to the motel. I hope they are done making love and I hope it makes her happy. I was suddenly possessed with the notion that I should hug everything on earth and that my own temporary euphoria would immediately heal all that I touched. Flower be well even though the cutworms have eaten off half your petals. Baby get up out of your crib and get rid of that leukemia. Dog regrow that leg you lost to a car.

None of it seemed likely and I came back to earth after imagining the difficulty of healing Tim's knot of scar tissue which like so many infirmities in friends one ceased noticing after a while. If other people didn't stare you wouldn't be reminded. Tito was almost envious and regarded it as a badge of courage. But I thought that every morning he shaved he must be reminded of the war though he never talked of it at all unless I brought up the subject and then he quickly dropped it. He said that when he was wounded it was only like a good knockout punch in a fistfight. But I had never fought much and hadn't been knocked out. He did say that he had gotten in a fight with a member of a helicopter crew over the matter of shooting cattle. It was bad enough shooting those scurrying human figures let alone cattle looking skyward in alarm. Yes it was true that prisoners being interrogated were occasionally pushed out the open door of a Sikorsky gunship at three thousand feet but Tim thought that was only part of war. Bad as it was it was more interesting than Georgia, and the re-up bonus was a big one.

I was finally nearing the motel. I stopped and lit a cigarette. The car was there and the room was dark. Tim had said he liked to screw with the lights on so I could assume that they were finished. He said Sylvia didn't like to make love with any light at all but she had gradually got used to it and if she had a few drinks would make love in front of the mirror. This was all said in Texas three or four days ago with Sylvia listening and looking out the window. They all know we are assholes. I turned the key in the lock and stepped in.

"Tim?" Sylvia said.

"No. It's me." I turned on a bed lamp. She was sitting with the sheet drawn up and her eyes were red and one side of her cheek was slightly swollen.

"He went looking for you. He didn't drive."

"It doesn't look like you guys had much fun." I was instantly struck by the stupidity of my statement.

"He said he doesn't want to sleep with me any more. He said I confuse him and that I only want him to marry me." Her voice was weary and flat. I began to wish that it wasn't so late and television was still on. I felt dull and sleepy and extremely tired of their frazzled entanglements. Romantic love was certainly our messiest invention. Wasn't there any way I could get back that stern glow I had in the tavern. I reached in my suitcase and got out the *Blaster's Handbook* and a pint of tequila.

"Take a drink and go to sleep." I handed her the pint and leaned down to kiss her forehead. She put her arms around my neck and we hugged, another one I couldn't heal. By her trembling I could tell that she was going to weep and I tried to get up. I murmured sweet comforting fatuities but she began sobbing anyway. Oh, Christ. I opened my eyes and looked down her bare back and watched my hands at her waist to see if they were going to do anything stupid. I ran a hand along her backbone then tucked in my chin to see her breasts against my shirt. A nipple was touching a small pearled button on my flowered cowboy shirt. The worm was going to turn so I tried to get away again.

"Sylvia, I can't say anything that will help." I was desperate about getting away. I held her shoulders and she lifted her face with those hazel eyes so pointlessly full of tears. "You should go home tomorrow. We'll put you on a plane and you'll be home in a few hours, at least to Atlanta. Rosie and Frank will drive up to get you." She paused a moment thinking it over and then began to cry harder, encircling her arms around my neck again.

"Sylvia!" I was pissed off now and wanted to get out of there. A plan evolved. I ran my hands between the sheet and her buttocks and began kneading them. What smooth skin. No effect though. I removed my left hand and forced it down between her legs letting the forefinger and then another enter her. She became very stiff in my arms and then slumped back on the bed. I followed the course of my arm down to my wrist and hand and then looked at her. She was wide-eyed but her face was incomprehensible. I moved my fingers. Perhaps a minute passed.

"Please don't." Her face was contorted.

I withdrew my hand and uncapped the tequila bottle. I took a swallow and passed it to her.

She gulped at it and shook her head. "It's awful," she said. She nearly smiled.

I quickly walked into the bathroom. It felt as if my head were about to blow off my shoulders like some old anarchist cartoon. In the shower I thought about Dexedrine and how in college if you dropped a few spansules to study you felt very alive but it was impossible to make love. Maybe Tim knows it but his kind of speed is even more violent. I'll talk to him but maybe he doesn't care. I had a terrible hard-on but the shock therapy had worked. For an instant I thought it might work too well.

When I got out of the shower her lamp was off but a street light outside made the tequila bottle visible and I took a final swallow.

"Are you sort of weird like Timmy?" Her voice had startled me.

"What do you mean?" I took an additional final swallow.

"Well, we really haven't made love for three or four months. Only that thing the whores do once or twice." Her voice was even and low.

"That's making love too," I said without much conviction. "He takes a lot of pills. If he stopped taking so many pills he would make love to you." I knew he varied his speed with Seconal which didn't help and at the slightest headache he would add a couple of Darvon to the stew. Christ.

"I know it's the pills but he could stop. We used to make love all the time. Even in San Diego in the hospital. I don't think he really wants me any more or he would stop."

"It's hard to stop." I felt foolish standing there in the dark dispensing counsel when I really wanted to get in her bed if only for a few minutes.

"I can see you're not very weird." I had been temporarily blinded from the light in the bathroom and thought the room was darker than it was. I was standing there with my hard-on visible if only dimly.

"I think the poor thing wants you very much, Sylvia." My mind was racing. "I almost wanted to rape you before. I'm tired of seeing you with no chance of having you. I love you and it's hard being around like a sad uncle all the time." My breath was racing now and I wished that we would hear Tim's key and put an end to the nonsense.

"I couldn't do that. I know you want to have me because I see the way you're looking at me all the time. Maybe I could do that other thing sometime."

I lay back on my bed then with my heart pounding. I smoked several cigarettes and could hear her steady breathing that meant she was asleep. I was still awake an hour after it got light when Tim slipped quietly in the door. I pretended to sleep but watched him sit back in a chair, prop his feet on the TV table, and promptly pass out. Where in Christ did he get those new boots in the middle of the night? They were pale blue and heavily tooled with steep heels. I'm sort of intelligent. I've got to get out of this mess. An awful case of heartburn from the tequila and lying here looking at Sylvia's sheet-draped rear which is aiming. Enter her de rerum natura as Lucretius. Ho ho, but the idea seizes until I dismiss it with the torrent of water and mud from a blown-out dam and running through the woods back to the car with the mud spattering on the trees and the fish free to go back to the main stream. I have struck. Opening the eyes and there's Sylvia. Women can't justly go to war as they disturb the planning. Tim snores on. The watch says seven. My too intelligent wife is getting up. My mother has my two degrees up on the wall. I have a closetful of mounted fish and a twelve-year fishing log. And that's about all I own I guess except all of those fly rods in the closet with the plaster fish we caught together. Mount no more fish. Let them go. Should break the rods and ascend into the good life.

A decade ago I even taught Sunday school. After I was saved. Couldn't interest the little buggers with anything but tales of missionaries being strangled by giant snakes and eaten by hyenas. God is not very interesting they thought. Compared to animals. Maybe I can retrieve my body from exhaustion and drink but also fish the Fraser and the south fork of the Flathead and the Madison and the Henry's Fork and the inlet of Hegben Lake. Shit my stomach burns. Tomorrow in the car

I'll tie up leaders with 4X and 5X tippets but also some that are heavier. We have no frying pan. Either buy a frying pan or let them all go, every single one. When they fight they build lactic acid and often die from it especially large tarpon that jump a dozen times with gill plates rattling and the water shedding as if they were hurled from an underwater catapult. I want to stand in that tower in the Marquesas and not know these people. Now the sheet is down a bit and I can see half her back. My hands slide down her back. She's so tight. The skin so smooth it is rare. I'll think about death to forget her. I'm blown up with the dam. They find my foot or head and then she is sorry. I hope. I wish I had put my face where my fingers were and that would have shocked her out of weeping fast. Maybe. I don't think I want her mouth but I do horribly though it seems improbable and far away. Only a service to which out of pity she yields. If we could cry like that we would truly clean out our heads almost at will.

CHAPTER

AT BREAKFAST which we had in the early afternoon I looked at
my maps. I was Timoshenko in exile; all of those lovely tactile
multicolored lines before me as I traced the best route north.
And the coy succession of inverted W's that meant the moun-
tainous Continental Divide. But there were disappointments
too; I knew the fabled Bighorn River near Crow Agency, Montana, was in reality only a muddy slough where a hundred
years before Custer's men had drained their frivolous blood.
Lucky Benteen. I've always been psychologically geared to retreat. Even without a recent advance, retreat is so often the
sensible course. We would take Route 89 north, not the best
route certainly but a route I had never been on and I was the
chief navigator. At every junction Tim would say "Which
way?" with an almost preposterous lack of interest. After con-
sulting a map I would hand it to Sylvia to fold. She was very
dexterous at it and would make the maps crisp and virginal
again.

My eggs were getting stiff and congealed and the coffee was
loathsome and served in stained plastic cups. Tim had given
Sylvia a half dollar for the jukebox and her choices were ruin-

ing my heady reconnaissance efforts. The first two songs were Merle Haggard's "Today I Started Loving You Again" and then the Conway Twitty-Loretta Lynn duet, "Lead Me On." Both maudlin, corrupt, causing an eerie wave of sentiment. I had danced in so many bars to both the songs with my face in a girl's neck and my hands lightly on her back. In Agua Prieta Sylvia had been a graceful dancer with her pelvis thrust ever so lightly against mine, and a smile however brief on her face. I lacked the native coordination to be a truly good dancer but Sylvia was marvelous.

Tim was rattling on in his usual speed rip about how he had bought these great Tony Lama boots off a drunk for only ten dollars and wonder of wonders they fit pretty well, maybe a bit loose but he could wear two pairs of socks and then they would be perfect only maybe a little hot and so on. He wasn't eating and I noticed that he was paler and had lost weight since the Keys. His arms looked less muscular though still powerful, but his eyes glittered and his face was drawn with exhaustion. Sleeping in a chair, then when we got up he washed down a couple of spansules from a new bottle when Sylvia was in the bathroom. He began another disconnected speech about a fire on a dirt stock car track where a friend of his had been burned badly only luckily not on the face when he hit a barrier and the gas tank hadn't been placed either properly or legally and he began to lose interest in stock cars when he heard his friend screaming. The bleachers were quiet and the other cars had stopped and everyone could hear the screaming as they extinguished the fire. Sylvia was looking down at her plate obviously realizing that Tim had been dropping his pills again. He plucked nervously at his scar when he talked and drank three or four cups of coffee, lighting one cigarette with another on the verge of going out.

A particular burned-grease smell had taken me away from the diner. At first I couldn't locate it but then I placed the smell in a small French restaurant on Ninth Avenue in the Fifties in New York. I ate lamb which they cooked rare and artichokes vinaigrette. Sometimes I would have sweetbreads. Then I would go to a movie or a concert or even an Off Broadway play. This was several years ago when I wanted very badly to be sophisticated. I wore cheaper imitations of the sort of clothing one could buy in the men's boutique at Bonwit's. This lust for the civilized even entered my fishing of that period: only eighteen-foot gut leaders and silk lines and very small fly patterns seemed appropriate, and English nylon waders. I nearly bought an umbrella one day. But that period of my life had passed, in fact had lasted only a few months. I could live for a week now on what I had once saved and then spent on a Côte Basque lunch for myself and some pretentious cunt.

What I frequently missed though was talking to bright people and also the sort of movie which so rarely reached the rural parts of the country. That Levantine gaze of Jeanne Moreau in *Jules and Jim* or Monica Vitti in sunglasses. But then I had gotten so generally strung out by urban life that I felt I must return to the "land" which proves even now to be a rather literary urging. The farmers who own and work the land scarcely ever sit around talking about the "land." I sort of knew this from my youth but had forgotten it. The land is good, my sister. That kind of thing. I noticed that the fishing was no longer as good as the old days and this drove me around the country in a veritable frenzy trying to cream the good fishing before it totally disappeared.

I was looking at their waists, then I noticed Tim and Sylvia were standing there waiting for me to get over my reverie. Sylvia in contrast to Tim looked so fresh in a short blue skirt and sleeveless white blouse and sandals. Her hair was drawn back in an unfashionable ponytail and her face showed no sign of last night's collapse. It occurred to me he must have slapped her when I remembered the swelling. But there is nothing quite so bad as not being able to get it up. You look at the goddamn thing and become hysterical over the way it works its own will, is contentious when you need it to be cooperative. And the girl, whoever she is, tries to be nice about it though you might have worked her up to the point that her face is a bleary mask. There's a toggle switch in the brain that we are not allowed to touch that runs the whole show. It seems unjust. And is. Faulty workmanship, God. Try again next time.

I dreaded the car. It was hot and when I put my suitcase in the trunk earlier the two cases of dynamite had all the attractiveness of two giant cysts. Toss them over in the shrubbery but they would be traced to us. They fell out of the trunk, officers, where bad guys had put them when we were drunk. Some dirty hippies probably. But who were hippies these days when a shoestore owner in Waco, Texas, might be mistaken for a Rolling Stone. I had heard these shoestore people talking in the Braniff Lounge at Love Field in Dallas the year before. One particularly odious type in a Bill Blass outfit said to a younger clean-cut type that he had expanded and was "grooving on my own thing." I contemplated walking over and smashing his head in with my aluminum fly rod case.

While I guided Tim out of Tucson I noticed that he was a good deal jumpier than usual and was tempted to ask him what kind of pills he scored in his middle-of-the-night wanderings. He was making an effort to be good humored though he was rather distant with Sylvia. I sat in the middle of the back seat and studied their heads. One didn't need to be telepathic to perceive what they were thinking about. Every few songs Tim would compulsively change the tape in the deck and it was beginning to put me on edge. He kept changing the volume and balance and it struck me that unless something good happened it would be a long and nasty day.

I reflected stupidly on how much everyone needed the night to give at least the appearance of a fresh start. I understood that we needed dreams to work out the kinks in our brains and that if we didn't dream for a long enough period, say a year, we were likely to go batty. I had lost my fair share of night; my mind helplessly rehearsed the scene with Sylvia and looking at the back of her head I wondered if she were thinking of it too. My fingers. And how her belly looked under the bed lamp. We forget how hot humans are and how physical. Ninety-eight and six tenths and damp. I allowed myself a long tremendously involved sexual fantasy about Sylvia and we were in Phoenix by the time it ended. I placed the whole thing in London to get rid of Tim. My imagination had so convinced my body that I was breathing hard and my groin stirred painfully. It was a letdown when she turned in her seat and started telling me that an aunt and uncle had lived in Phoenix for a year but had come back to Georgia for a lack of good work. I only looked at her sweet mouth and thought of all the uses I had just put her to. She was puzzled.

In the late afternoon somewhere between Flagstaff and Cameron a state trooper pulled us over. I saw the flasher first and exploded with a "Jesus" that startled Tim and Sylvia. Our minds seemed to zero instantly on the dynamite and we began to groan. I sat up straight so quickly I dumped the contents of my fly box on my lap. Tim took out his wallet as the trooper approached.

"We got our ass in a sling." Sylvia rolled her eyes at me and put her hand on his arm to steady him. "If he looks in the trunk we got our ass in a sling," Tim repeated.

"You were weaving back there." The trooper stooped taking Tim's license. He stared at Sylvia then at me. I was nervously busy putting the flies back in the box. "Fishing?" He moved his head further in the window and looked at my pile of leader spools and fly boxes.

"Yeah. We were down Guaymas. Now we're going up to

Wyoming and fish the Snake and the Clark's Fork." I thought my voice was quavery but he seemed not to notice.

"That's an awful big stone nymph." He picked up the fly and leaned back out of the window, examining the fly closely.

"I fish it deep with a high D line. Keep it." My voice relaxed a bit as the adrenalin subsided.

"No. I can't accept anything." He tossed me the fly and walked back to the squad car to check us out. He fiddled around for a few minutes.

"I don't think he called in," Tim said. The trooper was approaching again. He stuck his head in the window, glancing, I thought, at Sylvia's legs which she was crossing and uncrossing out of trepidation.

"I'll trade you this for that stone nymph." He handed me a vulgar-looking weighted streamer, an attractor pattern used mostly in discolored water.

"Fine with me. Take two. They're hard to get hold of."

"O.K. Be careful on this road. There's a lot of drunk Indians hereabout." He walked back to his car and made a U-turn heading back toward Flagstaff with incredible acceleration.

We sat there in silence for a few minutes. I reflected dully on a civil rights worker I had met once who said that when he drove through Mississippi he always had golf clubs in his station wagon though he didn't play golf. And the ultimate disguise for a big dope wholesaler would be a Ford pick-up with a camper towing a boat.

"We got to get rid of that fucking dynamite. We can get more in Idaho." I thought we weren't acting very professional for saboteurs. Tim quickly agreed and I looked at the map for a road that would turn off into the high desert country we were passing through.

"I thought he was real nice," Sylvia said. Tim began laughing. I had been upset with him all afternoon. He had driven erratically but had refused to give up the wheel. We had argued seriously for the first time: Tim wouldn't promise to keep the car below eighty and was further insulted when Sylvia sided with me after he swerved to miss some tumbleweed. I offered to get off in Flagstaff which served to slow him down but then at the fountain at a service station I watched him drop two more pills. We talked for a few minutes and he admitted he was out of control. It was apparent to both of us that we were both thinking of the trouble he and Sylvia had had in bed and I thought numbly about how crappy sex can be, how infinitely susceptible to not working well. But he said that last night hadn't really mattered except for his pride. He felt sorry for Sylvia and wished to God he knew how to stop her from loving him because he was sick to death of it. He punched me lightly on the shoulder, then and smiled his "everything fine now" smile. But only fifty miles further on he flipped again. He announced that he was sure Sylvia and I had screwed last night and didn't care but we could at least admit it. We were subjected to a long crazy tirade on women and how he preferred the tough whores he knew in L.A. or the Vietnamese girls, neither of whom ever whined or demanded marriage or tried to tell you what to do and they were great fucks too unlike certain women he knew. Sylvia said nothing but I offered that marriage was good enough, that I had been married for six years and that there had been some fine years. But he said why are you here or in Florida. A good question.

Now we had to get rid of the dynamite. It didn't matter much—I knew from my reading that there were better ways to blow a dam. It was merely too bad that Tito had fucked us out of the money. I directed Tim off a side road near Tuba City which though it was blacktop looked very deserted. We drove about a dozen miles on it, then turned up a dusty two-track and came upon a small shack behind a rock outcropping. The shack was empty and doorless and smelled badly of sheep. We put the dynamite in the corner, then stood looking out at the beautiful succession of mesas in the twilight and the thunderheads gathering above them that gave the air a yellowish cast with their backlight.

We had a violent argument: Tim wanted to set the dynamite off. Sylvia watched blankly from the door and I finally acquiesced out of curiosity. This after all could be rated as a trial run and I never had seen two cases of dynamite explode. Tim sent Sylvia back toward the car in case something went wrong. I served as a lookout while he fiddled with his pliers and the caps and a small roll of wire. When he was finished we walked down the hill toward Sylvia who waited a hundred yards below us. Tim ran to the car and got a large battery out of the trunk. Sylvia was grinning and I put my arm around her waist. She looked stunning with the yellow evening light shining on her face and hair and legs.

It began to sprinkle and the large sporadic raindrops raised little cones of dust. Tim spliced another roll of wire and we moved the car another hundred yards down to the blacktop while he followed on foot unrolling the wire. Sylvia was excited and swiveled in the seat watching Tim out the back window. Her panties were a gossamer black today and I momentarily forgot what we were doing. I ran my hand along her leg but she slapped it away though she was still smiling. I positioned the car and got out leaving it running. Tim told Sylvia to get back in the car. We talked for a moment looking nervously both ways on the road. Then I got in the back seat.

When it happened I knew I would remember it clearly until I died. Tim stood there cradling the battery in his arm and holding the wire with the other hand. He grinned at us, looking either like a maniac or the happiest man on earth. The hand with the wire moved and touched just as a battered old pick-up came over the hill toward us from the direction of Tuba City. For some reason I watched the truck draw closer rather than the explosion behind the rocks. The truck was perhaps a quarter mile away when the dynamite went off. Tim was in the car shifting when the shock waves hit and the incredibly spectacular noise that followed. Sylvia was screaming. Later it seemed that it sounded like a thousand of those Fourth of July buzz bombs at once. The tires burned and smoked and we saw the startled faces of three Indians as we passed the pick-up. They had stopped, straddling the center line, and Tim had to swerve to miss them. My skin prickled and I had forgotten to breathe. It was magnificent. Sylvia stopped screaming and turned around toward me still very wild eyed. Tim pushed the car up over a hundred and the wind roared in the windows.

"I shouldn't have dropped the fucking battery. My fingerprints are on the fucking battery." He slowed a trifle and we rolled up the windows.

"They'll never report it." I wasn't convinced but knew by the time they got turned around and to a telephone we would have an hour start. Besides they couldn't have got our license number. "I know we're good. They'll never report it. And nobody would believe them unless they came out and saw for themselves."

10

THERE were magpies on the roof and bluejays somewhere in the trees nearby. I had heard some animal scratching underneath the floor and each time I awoke to the scratching I would have to focus on the yard light until I remembered where I was. For the first time we slept separately. The small cabins only had one bed but they were very cheap; they were musty and smelled strongly of pine, and pitch still oozed fragrantly from the cracks in the boards. It had been a very cool night and I got up at dawn to adjust the electric wall heater.

Out the window in the still first light I could see dew on the car. The cabins and the store were dark but the owner's dog, a shepherd-collie cross, shuffled around the yard and drank from the creek which was the border of the yard before the forest began. He looked into the forest and barked once. I woke often and lorded in my privacy imagining that I was far up in some mountain fastness and had never had anything to do with blowing a Navajo shed to dust and splinters with two cases of dynamite. But I couldn't dismiss the shed—the noise had been too palpable, a steady roar that imitated itself in successive waves and layers. A bit of the overkill but we got rid of the stuff.

We had driven up to Page, quickly eaten, and checked into the cabins. Tim seemed very near collapse. I talked him into three Seconals and he was asleep by ten. I sat with Sylvia on their porch steps for a little while then kissed her good night. She was shivering and sounded drained as we talked but still quite excited. I had lost all fear of being caught and when we said good night I walked over to the store and bought a pint of whiskey. The owner was a pleasant asthmatic retiree from Mansfield, Ohio. We chatted in the dark about bass fishing and shared a few pulls from the bottle. He had worked in a steel mill until his lungs went bad and wished that he had never seen Mansfield, Ohio, but had been born right here near Page. He allowed that the Glen Canyon dam had been good for his business but he had liked it better before. I agreed as lakes and reservoirs usually bore the shit out of me. I asked him about a proposed Grand Canyon dam but he said that it was only a realtor's dream that got a lot of publicity. Of course the Army Corps of Engineers would be glad to build a dam even if there were no water within a hundred miles. He laughed a lot and appeared sorry when I said I had to get some sleep. I didn't finish a whole drink before I dropped off despite the lumpy mattress and damp sheets. I telephathically invited Sylvia over but she failed to materialize.

By mid-morning, nearly twelve hours later, I still hadn't got out of bed. The exhaustion was cumulative; I couldn't remember sleeping eight hours since several days before we left Key West. Then I heard the car leave and I remembered that Tim had said there was something that needed fixing in the timing or the distributor. I got into the old metal shower stall and convinced myself that the cold water was invigorating. Snow has to be wonderful if that's all you have. I finished off last night's drink and shuddered. I would go on the wagon.

I heard a knock and let Sylvia in. She had brought me coffee and a doughnut from the store. I drank it holding my towel skirt together with my other hand. She didn't look good sitting there so primly on the folding chair at the end of the bed.

"Good morning, beautiful."

She didn't look up. "Tim sort of flipped in the middle of the night for about an hour. Then he took more pills and was O.K. Only this morning his head hurt so much I thought he was going to cry."

"Well at least we got some sleep. That should help." I put down my coffee and patted her shoulder. She leaned against my leg.

"Are you trying to comfort me again?" She smiled and stood up. I hugged her, still holding my towel. "Your towel is wet."

"Oh, fuck you." I sat down on the bed. I only wanted to be kind I thought.

She stepped over and ran her hand through my hair. I stared glumly at her wrist and hips. How could she be a foot away and still so distant.

"Why would you cheat on a friend?" Her smile had become quizzical.

"We don't have to cheat but we could at least tease ourselves a little."

She laughed and lifted my chin and kissed me for a second but when I ran my hand along her leg and tried to prolong the kiss she backed away. "How do you tease?"

I searched for a good answer that would keep the atmosphere light. "Oh you know, neck and pet a little like they used to in Fred Astaire-Ginger Rogers movies or like Natalie Wood and James Dean. Nothing serious. I've been a whole week without any woman at all and it's impossible." I thought this might disarm her.

"What about those whores?" She became serious.

"They don't count." I knew then for the hundredth time in

my life that I couldn't talk a girl into my bed. I felt clumsy and contemplated a total clown act that might send her shrieking from the cabin.

"They took care of Timmy all right."

"Why don't you go away." I was appalled by my directness but continued. "I'm sick of looking at your sweet ass which you're welcome to save as long as you want. You know I love you. You love Timmy and he doesn't screw you and you know what it feels like. I feel the same way and I wish the fuck I'd never laid eyes on your goddamn dumb hillbilly face. You know goddamn well nothing is going to happen for you but your stupid cow brain can't figure it out and rather than be nice to someone who loves you you sit around crying over someone who doesn't. You're beautiful but you're an out an out stupid cunt. Period."

I knew I had gone too far and even in my anger I felt ashamed. Her face had a strangled look and she stood there with her hands held stiffly at her sides.

I got up and hugged her. "I'm sorry and I'll never say anything like this again. I'm sorry." I dropped my arms and she turned and walked out the door.

I lay back in the bed listening to the magpies and sipping from my pint of whiskey which I thought I'd like to throw. But drinking would help more than throwing. That should be the end of that. It would be hard for her to be even friendly to me now. I was overwhelmed with regret—being her brother or uncle was a little bit better than nothing no matter how difficult it had become. Then I lived out a fantasy of us living together and tried to convince myself how ill-suited we were for each other. What would she be like in New York or San Francisco and would she look as beautiful and graceful. Yes. No question about it. She would be a perfect wife but I already had a perfect wife. What then? But loving someone, especially at first, never seems to involve any questions. Maybe it would help if we could make love, if only once. But that was a lie. The two women I had loved the best in my life were my worst lovers and it made no difference. I suddenly envied the crudity of my friends though I often seemed on the verge of it myself. Percy Shelley. Or Keats. Indeed. I lay there in an utter funk. Then Sylvia walked back in without knocking and I quickly covered myself for a change.

"I brought you a sandwich and a beer." She sat down on the folding chair.

"Thanks." I lay back with the sandwich on my chest. "I'm very sorry."

She turned in the chair and ran her hand idly along my foot. She seemed very far away and I felt that from then on I would try to make her happy no matter how difficult it was for me. She wasn't tough enough to be hurt badly and recover as I did so habitually. If I left now I would be over it all in a month. I felt sure of that though I didn't feel up to trying it.

"You shouldn't be sorry. It makes me feel good that you love me." She got up and took my hand. "I think I'm quite old fashioned and the way you and Timmy are scares me. Timmy tells me to make love to you but I think it would just make him feel free." She sat down on the edge of the bed. "Why don't you eat your sandwich? He should be here soon and he'll want to go."

"Kiss me. And I'll eat this."

She was puzzled for a moment, then leaned down to me. "You don't look like a movie star so how can I pretend we're in the movies?" She lifted half the sandwich and offered me a bite. I grabbed her wrist but she pulled away so I loosened my grip. "If I'm going to kiss you you can't grab me."

"Cross my heart." I held my hands along my sides as if I were standing at attention. She put the sandwich on the night-stand, then pulled the sheet up my belly further. "This is like playing doctor and I'm twenty-eight years old. You're going to pay big for this someday."

"Maybe." She paused. "You meant everything you said to me, didn't you? I'm probably very dumb, not like your wife or other girls you like." Now she was resting against my chest and her face was only a few inches from mine. I wasn't absolutely sure she was serious but guessed that she was. I glanced down her blouse and smelled jasmine and saw how the pressure raised her breasts.

"Please." She kissed me then and the kiss continued for several minutes. I broke my promise and slid her entire weight on me with my right hand. I raised her skirt tentatively but she continued the kiss. I brushed my hands over her buttocks and the simple cotton panties and then clenched each of them. The kiss became more open-mouthed and deeper. I pulled the sheet down and let my cock rest against her and then I lowered it and pushed her down so that it bored against her. I opened my eyes and saw that hers were open too. I swiveled her hips against myself, then had to pause for fear of coming. I ran my hands under her panties until the tips of my fingers touched my cock which was pressed in, impeded only by the cloth. Then we heard the car.

Sylvia jumped up and drew the bedclothes over me, quickly put the sandwich back on my chest and the beer in my hand. She smoothed her skirt, grabbed the *Blaster's Handbook* off the nightstand and sat back down on the folding chair just as Tim walked in.

"At it again?" He was grinning and looked a lot better.

"I've tried hard but I think she must be frigid." I took a huge bite out of the sandwich and a swig of the beer. "Get the car fixed?" I nearly choked on the flat beer and wanted an Academy Award for acting. My poor cock hadn't begun to wilt under the bedclothes so sudden was the action.

"Yeah. The timing was off. There's nothing in the Flagstaff paper about the blast so I guess we're safe. Get ready and we'll get the fuck out of this pop stand." He turned to Sylvia. "Get me something to eat and a six-pack."

Tim sat down on the chair when she left. He began babbling about the mechanic he had met in Page who used to be a racing mechanic just like Tim's dad but mostly around Riverside in California. Then he started racing motorcycles and busted himself up pretty badly. I stretched and gave a false yawn waiting for my hard-on to subside so I could get up without suspicion.

"Haven't you tried to fuck her?" He was looking at me with just an edge of coldness.

"No. Would you try to fuck a woman of mine?" I gave him a hard stare that I hoped concealed any guilt.

"Depends on what she looked like," he said with amusement in his voice but that changed. "You should cut the shit though. I told her we were all done and whether or not you want her is your business." He drummed his blue boots against the end of the bed. "Give me a drink."

"But you just can't trade her off like that," I said passing him the pint.

He popped a pill, then drank. "Guess not. I don't want her on my hands any more and I like you. You would be better to her than I have. We used to be great but now I don't feel anything any more and there's no good reason to feel I do." The color in his face rose. "I wasn't going to see her again when we met in Key West. I was trying to figure out where I wanted to go in South America. Then when we decided to come out here and practically had to drive right through town it seemed like a good idea."

"Did you tell her that?" I started dressing and decided I wanted a fancy pair of boots like Tim's.

"Only about a dozen times. She thinks I don't love her because I drop all those pills. I told her that was nonsense. Sure we might fuck a lot but that never changed my mind in the past. When this is over I'm going to get the hell out of the country. I can ship on a motor schooner to Venezuela with a guy I know and make more on a load of grass than I could in ten years' working." He was buzzed up now. "But if you don't even like her there's nothing you can do about it."

"I like her a lot but she treats me like a brother. I think she would never do anything with me because that would let you take off scot free." A quarter of an hour before the brother had been a bit loose with the sister.

"Well it's too bad for you because I'm going to take off anyway and she has a great body and you would like her. You're always looking at her." He was pacing around the room laughing as I zipped up my suitcase.

"She's nice but she's not really my type. I'm like you. I don't want anyone to depend on me."

We left the cabin and I waved to the owner who was standing near his single gas pump. Sylvia sat on the car fender with the six-pack and a sack of food. She was drinking a Dr Pepper and when we approached she greeted us as if nothing had happened. We agreed that since we had come this close we should take a look at the Grand Canyon even though it lacked a trace of a dam. But we didn't think we could take the chance of driving back through Cameron and over to the south side of the Canyon which I knew was the best way to look at it. Instead we headed for Jacob's Lake and then down toward North Rim. I was oddly depressed by the immensity of the landscape. If you were to live here there would be a long period of adjustment and perhaps you would never get used to it.

At Navajo Bridge we threw stones down into the Colorado and I had vertigo almost to the point of nausea. I wondered how the Indians ever got back and forth across the river let alone adapted themselves to the austerity of the landscape which seemed to shrink the human to a perhaps more accurate scale. Sylvia was delighted and Tim as usual was concentrating on making good time.

During the entire afternoon of fooling around North Rim I brooded about Sylvia. I had a more than a mild case of lover's nuts from our kiss and felt stupidly young and foolish. And put upon. I had slept too long and that caused a foggy sort of displacement. I walked around in a sensual haze and later could barely remember looking at the Canyon with any interest other than to wish I was a Havasupai Indian living down at the bottom. I was fatigued with trotting around like a pitifully horny dog. I was purposely distant with her, and her gaiety over the scenery disgusted me. Tim mostly concentrated on the idea that it would be impossible to blow any dam large enough to cross the Colorado unless you owned a squadron of B-52s. At dinner while Tim was in the toilet Sylvia reached for my hand and said that she was sorry we had been interrupted, that it had been "fun."

CHAPTER

11

TRAVELING north through Utah our plot began to take a more definite shape. And the optional methods narrowed down to the fusion of kerosene and bags of nitrogen fertilizer, both less traceable than the more stagy dynamite. I had read about the method years before in an outdoor magazine where it was recommended for making instant ponds in low lying areas for the propagation of ducks. And assuming some caution, it was safe. Three or four bags would make a hole as large as an average bomb crater. We would have to double up a bit on quantity because we wouldn't have time to bury the bags. And we would buy the material in Montana and rent a small U-Haul so that it would be extremely unlikely that we would be caught by the usual circumstantial route. Perhaps we would try the method in Montana with a bag or two to see if we judged it as adequate. I was sure but Tim wondered why more people weren't using it. I said because everyone wasn't us. In Michigan a landowner could illegally dam up a feeder stream but he would only be fined fifty dollars and the dam stayed. I began to get the holy glow I had in the tavern in Tucson. And Tim suggested that maybe we should blow up a dozen dams or fifty or a hundred and make a real mark for ourselves. Why stop at one or two? It was infectious and I saw us as the equivalent of the Resistance in France moving around the country committing just acts of sabotage. We talked on for hours in the Utah night with Sylvia dozing prettily. At a gas station while Tim was out of the car I kissed her awake and she smiled sleepily but it reminded me horribly of kissing my daughter good night. I didn't need such thoughts now when I would have to summon up all of my not very considerable nerve for what we were going to do. We were getting uncomfortably close to having to actually carry out our plans that had been made so blithely. It was ominous. I had immoderately thrilling visions of my picture in post offices where the FBI posters are tacked in sheaves: WANTED FOR UNLAWFUL ACTS OF SABOTAGE . . . CONSIDERED ARMED AND EXTREMELY DANGEROUS . . . TO BE APPROACHED WITH GREAT CAUTION.

We began discussing escape routes now that we had become so notorious in our conversation. The Yucatán or Quintana Roo sounded good but so did the island of Cozumel where I could fish out my dark exile. Or Cartagena in Colombia which I suggested to Tim not because I knew what was there but because the name sounded good. Tim preferred the Far East. If I would only get a taste of the kind of action he had had on R and R in Hong Kong and Tokyo. But I declined as there wasn't any good fishing on my terms in the Far East.

So we played on with explosions and locations through the night. Not petty but giant crime and the map freakery involved in such names as Temuco, Vera Cruz, Belize, Alexandria, Trinidad, Cabo San Luca and so on. I told him about the good month I had in Salinas, Ecuador, how the fishing was exquisite and you could live very cheaply there. The girls were pretty too though you had to be careful as shankers were prevalent. But Tim's notions were more movie oriented and swashbuckling.

We would need a fortune off a bank robbery or some vague huge dope deal. Then we would live stylishly in the tropics, gamble a lot, stay stoned and wear white linen suits. Our plans began to fall apart a bit but we finally reached a compromise with the Caribbean where both fishing and the high life were possibilities though the location was less redolent with mystery than some of the other places.

Sylvia would occasionally wake and change a tape and say something though we were too busy to pay any attention to her. She didn't obviously appear in any of Tim's plans and she seemed to sense this. But frequently in our endless talk I would place her in a hotel room with me, or in a boat or she would be on the beach waiting for me when I returned in the evening. I could see her slightly darkened by the sun which would emphasize the greenness in her eyes and bleach her hair. But so often my power of fantasy would lapse and I would either see us caught and imprisoned or, worse yet, Sylvia would disappear. I could not bear to think of the event in the cabin and how I would have been in her, in fact was in her almost, were it not for a millimeter of cotton. Perhaps that was as close as I would get. And it somehow began to matter less. The closeness was enough and brought on that strange sickness of the heart and throat and loins and though it might have been fatigue made me feel weepy at the thought of it. For a silly instant I knew I would kill to get her and what I would do with her was irrelevant.

We were still barreling along at dawn. Sylvia and I kept at Tim until he agreed to stop at a motel. We found a vacancy just over the Wyoming border near Evanston though the owner was cranky at being waked early. But the motel was scabby enough with just a few cars in front so he needed the business. I stood out in front of our unit for a half hour smoking cigarettes; I didn't want to see Sylvia in any state of undress, and even more I didn't want to see her get in bed with Tim while

I lay there three feet away paralyzed with jealousy.

Now in the first light, standing in the gravel parking lot, all of my berserk enthusiasm, fed by Tim's speed talk and my imagination and a dozen tapes in the deck, had vanished. The landscape was bleak and the air already warm. I thought about the false power of music, the insanely dead-end kind of romanticism it promoted. If you listened to the Stones at high volume long enough you invariably had some sort of sympathy for the devil. And hearing that Dylan-Cash duet you wanted to travel north and find a girl at a county fair. Tim's apparent favorite which I had begun to dread was Joplin's "Get It While You Can" which seemed unequaled in modern music for sheer relentless desperation. Millions listen to these songs and unless they are utter dullards they must be affected by them. Maybe it's good. What did the previous generation get out of Perry Como and Andy Williams and Rosemary Clooney? But often it seemed the passion was excessive and the music transliterated the passion so accurately that you couldn't help but be convinced. Merle Haggard always made me want to get drunk. The Cream or The Who or The Grateful Dead made me want to get stoned while with Dolly Parton I wanted to fall in love. June Carter seemed to beckon from Jackson, Mississippi, and Patsy Cline from Nashville. No wonder that most people prefer weak, sappy music.

When I entered the room Tim was lying on his back staring at me. He childishly pushed down the sheet to reveal Sylvia again in those white lollipop panties sleeping deeply on her stomach. Then he pushed them down and I gave him the finger and bolted for the bathroom. Great sense of humor. But I had convinced him that she meant nothing in particular to me. He was merely being playful.

Years ago I had read D. H. Lawrence and become convinced that he had the right attitude toward sex. But it was hard to avoid acting out the depths of one's own sexual neuroticisms, the perhaps inevitable arrested development. Somehow I became convinced that people who lived in cities and the Frenchmen and Italians seemed less guilty than those of us who had grown up in the small Calvinist backwaters. Probably no changing now. Or not much. The teenagers appeared to be escaping some of it.

I looked long and closely in the mirror for signs of incipient age and decay. Twenty-eight. Four times seven. Your life is supposed to change dramatically every seven years they say. Who says. The stars of course. We're in less than intimate contact I think. My throat hurts from smoking and my head from drinking and my ass from riding and the rest of me from Sylvia. My interest in life weakened again at a rapacious rate. It disappeared in fact while I brushed my teeth. Suicide was a thought that consistently held vitality.

Back in the room Tim was asleep with a pillow over his eyes; a ray of the early morning sun stretched across his pillow and vanished into Sylvia's hair. He hadn't covered her with the sheet and her bottom was still frighteningly bare. I tried to pretend it was someone else as I treated myself to a look. It was definitely faultless. I would gladly die upon it in a marathon effort. An Elizabethan suicide. She moved a little which opened her. Too much to take right now or at any time. Global. Now a fly ticked against the window and a truck passed. But I stood there long enough so that there was some question whether I was capable of moving. Early danger signal. Their breathing had joined the single fly, my heartbeat, and the hole left by the truck. For a moment I thought I might be able to hear the ray of sun that was lengthening across Sylvia's hair. I stared at her body so long that the strength of my perceptions weakened and the bed and the entire room became flat as a magazine photo. I became dizzy but discovered that I had ceased breathing.

Before I got in bed I dropped twenty milligrams of Valium,

surely a chickenshit drug compared to Tim's specialties, but perhaps it would get me some sleep. While waiting for its effect I tried to meditate on fishing. Tomorrow I might get a few hours on the Green—rather today—anyplace else I would have been up an hour by now for trout. On salt water you had to wait for the light, for the sun to climb enough so that it wouldn't reflect off the water which was usually around nine o'clock in the morning. At least in flats fishing where the skill depended so much on vision and the movement of the tides in the shallow water where it was so easy to confuse a fish with the configuration of the bottom. You might stand all day on the casting deck of a skiff and only get two or three shots at tarpon. The same if you were bonefishing. And in May it would be so hot that the sweat invariably got in your eyes and trickled down your belly and into your crotch and down your legs. But a day might come when you saw a hundred big tarpon in a single school wandering across a flat in three feet of water toward your staked skiff. The water was so thin that the silver backs and dorsals of the larger fish showed above the water and the fish would spook each other playfully. You hoped that another boat wouldn't appear, or a flock of gulls or pelicans or man-of-war birds to frighten them. No matter that most of them weighed over a hundred pounds, the tarpon still seemed constantly wary of birds which perhaps fed on their kind when the fish were small. It could be awful waiting, especially when you saw them coming three or four hundred yards away so that by the time they reached casting distance you were a basket case. But if you were lucky you might hook one or two of them if your first rig broke and you had another rod ready. If the hook was set well you might decide to fight the fish to the boat which often took more than an hour. Usually you purposely broke the leader after the tarpon made his inevitable succession of wild jumps that never failed to astound you with their strength and power.

Still awake but I could feel the first soft nuzzling of the Valium in my brain and limbs. Something like hashish only more soporific. And boring. Odd that suicide can be inadvertent or we don't recognize quite what we are doing. It's always been easy to dismiss the shotgun across the lap, the brief temptation to hurl from Navajo Bridge the other day my body not the rock, or to miss the abutment on the freeway that looked sort of attractive.

On the Yellowstone north of Livingston I fished one evening while in the middle of a severe strep infection. The high fever caused intermittent spells of dizziness so that I would have to grab something to avoid falling down. In my cabin I was either soaked with sweat or dry and burning. A doctor had cauterized my throat but it still hurt too much to get any whiskey past the raw parts. I had been in a severe depression for a year, so severe in fact that I no longer noticed my wife, daughter, dog. I had no interest in sex and when I would travel I had difficulty in remembering the sights I saw, meals eaten. I awoke one morning with my wife in a bedroom in an inn about thirty miles from London and said something that betrayed my state of mind so that she became very frightened—I had simply forgotten that we were in England.

So that evening in Montana I drove to a part of the Yellowstone just above where the river enters a small canyon for three miles and the cliffs are sheer. If you went under in your waders the chances of drowning were excellent. It would be hard to miss, the water was so turbulent and swift, and the shore held no place that was not solid rock. When I walked from my car to the river I had to sit down three or four times, and I fell when I first stepped into the river in a channel facing a sandbar. The main power of the river was beyond the sandbar and I cast from the sandbar on the spit that faced downstream toward the canyon. I took several good fish with no pleasure and still did not understand what I intended to do. I stepped into the water in the lee of the bar until the cold water reached my waist, then I slowly waded toward the main force of the current. I think I gulped air in anticipation of going under and the sharp pain in my throat brought me to full consciousness of what I was doing. My panic was instant and the surge of energy was incredible. I struggled back to the sandbar and lay there for an hour watching the evening sun move up the cliffs and the swallows dart in and out of their crannies. I saw a prairie falcon skitter along the top edge of the cliff looking for a meal. When it was dark I made my way back to the car and drove into town where I drank until I was comatose despite the pain of swallowing.

I woke up to laughter and pig noises. Tim had Sylvia around the waist at the foot of the bed. I covered myself for security.

"She wants a shower and I want to get to hell out of here." Then he oinked and snorted against the back of her neck. "Jesus you smell too good for a shower." He oinked down her back while she wriggled to get away. "I don't want to wait a fucking hour." He hauled her over to my bedside. "Smell her for Christ's sake."

"Smells like a manure pile," I said snorting loudly which made me cough. "Manure's fine for breakfast though." Sylvia kicked at me and I grabbed her foot to avoid injury.

"You're squeezing too hard!" Tim's arms were around her waist tightly.

"No shower or I'll take off your pants in front of this sex maniac." She struggled harder still laughing and he turned her toward him and got another hold. "De-pants her, sex maniac. She got me while I was sleeping and thinking about someone else."

I saw that Sylvia was blushing and I got out the other side of the bed and went into the bathroom. Well, they made love or at least she did. Glad I wasn't awake for that one. Thank

Valium. I turned on the shower full blast and, happy for a change, began singing my college fight song for no particular reason: "Close beside the winding cedars stands a college known to all; / Their specialty is winning and those Spartans play football," I brayed. Then Tim burst through the shower curtain still holding Sylvia.

"Glad to have you aboard," I yelled and continued the song in the spirit of the event. They were between me and the opening in the middle of the stream of water.

"Let's soap this pile of shit down." Tim took the soap from my hand. Sylvia stood between us with any escape route blocked by Tim. "This rapist needs cleaning up." He began soaping her front vigorously. She was braless but still had her panties on but then he knelt and pulled them down her legs. "Here, you soap the back." He handed me the soap and I began scrubbing. It was freaky enough that I didn't feel the least bit excited.

"She seems pretty clean." I was only halfway down her back but didn't have the heart to continue.

"All the way, chickenshit!" Tim was laughing with his face streaming with water. Sylvia turned and sort of rolled her eyes so I continued lathering and handed Tim the soap and he began washing himself. I let my hand linger unnecessarily between her legs but she didn't move. I began to tremble and the whole thing began to lose its humor.

"I'll bet you ten dollars he's got his hand up your ass," Tim said rinsing his face.

"No he hasn't," she said. She deftly moved from my hand and past Tim out of the shower.

PART
III

12

I HAD LOST all of my uncontrollable melancholy of the night before. Tim had agreed to stopping to fish for a while and Sylvia bought food and drinks for a picnic. And as we moved further north in Wyoming we finally escaped a week's worth of oppressive heat. But I suspected Tim wanted to slow down for the same reason I did—after our long burst of verbal energy expended in detailed planning, the future which was to be painted with a series of explosions began to appear as excessively close. Almost around the next curve on the highway. A drunk is heading for us at a hundred miles per hour. But maybe he felt nothing of this and I was only projecting my own weak-kneed sense of caution. I thought he was trying to cut down his pill intake, something he was accomplishing by drinking an endless succession of cans of Coors beer. We had no way to keep the beer cool so we bought it a six-pack at a time and drank quickly. The only sour aspect of the day was his teasing of Sylvia. He prattled on how he had never taken advantage of a drunk or drugged or otherwise incapacitated woman, only to have his own sleeping body misused. At first she laughed about it and said she had been half asleep herself and had dreamed they were back in the hospital bed in San Diego which had been for her, oddly enough, a happier time. But he didn't let up and she resorted to staring wordlessly out the window. I intermittently hated his needling but sometimes it became funny. I tried to help by changing the subject at every opportune lapse in the conversation. He would get interested in, say, certain structural aspects of earthen dams. But they were fairly simple and didn't hold attention. All that you had to do was blow a large enough trough and the force of the backed-up water would work for you sweeping the rest of the dam away.

It was so easy to become depressed with Sylvia's vulnerability. It was the same set of feelings I got when my daughter had a toothache or a bad earache. I would hold her three-year-old body weighing only thirty pounds and rock her; her face would be flushed with the fever and her eyes dull with pain. You wanted very badly to assume the pain for her and after many hours of it the depression would turn into anger.

In a pond in a gravel pit I had once helped dive for a drowned child. There was a newspaper reporter clicking pictures and in my nightmares about the event there was always the sound of the camera clicking. A friend that had found the child on the pond's bottom kept yelling that "she's cold." A few of the spectators had the dignity to run back to their cars but most stayed looking down at their shoes while the mother screamed. I was sixteen at the time and went to the drive-in movie that night with my girl friend. I sat there dumbly watching a giant ant attack some explorers but kept remembering the child's eyes had been open and when she was first brought to the surface I felt thrilled because she must be alive. I thought she was looking at me. I drank nearly a case of beer and my girl friend had to drive home.

We made several turns off the main road before I found what I thought was a fishable stretch of the Green combined with a good place to picnic. Tim was mildly irked because it all looked like water to him and he was sure that I was putting him on. But much of the water was wide, swift and shallow and I was looking for a stretch of the river that had deep pools where I might coax up a large fish in the midday glare. Sylvia set out the picnic but I declined to eat until I fished for a while.

I had an absurdly good time; though I lacked waders and couldn't reach some of the rises further out in the river I quickly became less finicky and walked into the river with my trousers and shoes on. The water was so cold it numbed my legs painfully so I would get out every ten minutes and stomp around to return my circulation. Most of the fish were smaller rainbows but they were beautifully colored and good fighters aided as they were by the strong current. I was struck again as I had been for years by how my fishing so hypnotically wiped the slate clean again though only for as long as I was in the river. For a few hours though all problems—money, sex, alcoholism, generalized craziness—disappeared in concentrating on the flow of water, the likely places for feeding trout to be, the clear current or in the eddies next to the grassy banks or behind the large rocks and boulders that broke the water's surface, forming pockets behind them that always seemed to hold a fish or two.

"Can I look at it?" It was Sylvia and she was seated on a rock not twenty feet behind me. I was both startled and irritated having been caught on the verge of giving a tiny rainbow a kiss before I released it.

"Yes. Of course." I waded over quickly. "I have to let it go fast or it will be hurt."

"It's pretty. Do they all have that pink stripe?"

"All the rainbows do." I stooped and gently released the fish in the slow water by the bank. It paused, moving its gills laboriously, then darted back out into the current. I was reminded rather painfully of my problem. Sylvia had her knees drawn up and was resting her arms and chin on them. If I didn't stand quickly I would stay there forever watching the way her inner thighs vanished into her crotch. Why did they bother wearing skirts at all?

"Go ahead and fish. I just want to watch." She let one foot trail in the water. Now the view was even better and my face felt stupidly hot when I thought of the shower of a few hours ago.

"No, I'm getting cold and a little hungry. Where's Tim?" I sat down on the sand beside her rock and lit a cigarette.

"He's been drinking a lot and fell asleep." I turned away from her thigh which was only a foot from my face. I almost wanted to burn it with my cigarette. What a false problem. I would become a monk of violence and blow myself up—troublesome cock and brain full of romance—in a single deliciously orange explosion. All of the peace of fishing had dissipated.

"Let's go up on the bank and make love." I scarcely believed I was saying it.

"I don't feel like it right now," she said as if my request and her denial were an everyday occurrence.

"I guess you took care of that while I slept." She stared down at me angrily and I grabbed her hand and squeezed it as if I were trying to joke. She sighed deeply.

"I was dreaming and when I was really awake he pushed me away and didn't even finish." She stood up and waded out into the river up to her knees but quickly got back out. "God it's cold. How can you stand it?"

"I couldn't." My legs were finally beginning to get warm. I gathered courage and caressed her thigh with my hand as she stood next to me. "Sylvia I'm not bragging but I'm sure I could make love to you until you were absolutely sick of it."

"It's strange but I thought both of you were going to make love to me in the shower. I was scared and didn't think you were going to let me go." She messed up my hair as I raised my hand further up the thigh.

"I wanted to." Then the car horn beeped. Jesus. The second time that bastard has interrupted. She laughed as the horn echoed down the river mixing with the roar of water. I pulled her down with force and she collapsed across my lap. I kissed her and pushed her dress up to her waist but when I let the kiss which seemed returned go she bit my finger and jumped up out of reach.

"Maybe the next time we have a chance." I sat there in my wet trousers doubting the eventuality of everything.

Selective dolor: the largest boulder which was directly across the river from me caught and deflected the water with the noise of a giant kettledrum. When she left, there was this wish to become the riverbed or a rock, something so slight as one of those thousands of planes of sun entering a ripple. Trapped. I heard Tim gun the car and still did not move. An otter appeared on the far bank but vanished when I waved. I was sated with the West and wanted to be on some other riverbank, say the Neva embankment in Leningrad when it was St. Petersburg. Perhaps Peter the Great would be walking along the path on an evening stroll and I would wave to him like I did the otter but then Peter vanished with the horn. I walked to the car in an utter numb boredom with forests, rivers, mountains, cars, Tim and Sylvia. Especially the unremitting lewdness she caused in my head so that the only interesting alternative to this lewdness was to blow up a dam. Two choices, both of which you had become committed to. As I drew near the car I imagined myself sitting on a terrace in sixteenth-century Rapallo drinking a pitcher of wine: I weighed three hundred, had a huge goiter, and my children scuffled in the dirt at my feet. Reality pudding.

"Sylvia said you made a pass at her." Tim was glancing in the rearview mirror.

"Oh, Timmy, shut up." His head jerked toward her.

"Yeah I did. I offered her a hundred dollars." I wanted to interrupt any fight before it started. "I was either going to borrow it from you or write a bad check." I passed them a joint that I had found in one of my fly boxes. Peaceful medicine I hoped. I thought it was from a friend's batch that had been mildly diced with opium. Should quiet him down.

"But I said I'm not worth a hundred dollars which is much more than you guys paid those beauties in Mexico," Sylvia joined in. "So I said twenty dollars is more than enough and I'll give it to Timmy for gas money."

"She's not worth twenty dollars even for around the world. There was this girl in Saigon that could pick up a silver dollar with her pussy." We had reached the main road and Tim was punctuating his talk by speed shifting.

The marijuana began to take effect and we all lapsed into joking. I tried to make up an original English folk song but it came out something like "Dingaling ding ding derry dery dery dog dodo" and it was booed. So much for a songwriting career. Tim told a longish story about how as a child he guarded his dad's toolbox at the big races where his dad acted as a racing mechanic. Sometimes on the infield near the track where the pit crews worked it would be a hundred thirty degrees. His dad had been one of the best mechanics until he lost a thumb and forefinger to a fan belt then retired to his small repair garage in Valdosta. Tim missed seeing the big track action and decided he wanted to be as famous as Junior Johnson or David Pearson or Cale Yarborough so he built up his Mercury in high school and ran around southern Georgia on weekends lying his age and racing. His football coach asked him to quit during the season so Tim had quit football where he had played both end and linebacker. He had gone to Georgia Tech because he wanted to build a super car. Sylvia began talking about a football game where the first teams had both been thrown out for fighting and spectators had run on the field to join the fight. Tim added that it had been more fun than any football game he had ever played in because their coach whom he hated had been hit over the nose with a helmet and bled like a chicken with its head chopped off.

But I had dropped far back into my own head and the little trip had become a bummer. Their talk seemed to indicate a direct connection with the past and what they were now. This was startling and I felt envious. There was a shrill phenomenology in thinking about my own life in comparison—the "we are one thing because we are not another" sort of confusion: I am only here near Bondurant, Wyoming, because I am not in the Marquesas fishing.

I said something crossing the street. I said something to Sylvia in a cabin and we nearly made love like cataleptic fifties teenagers. A large trout didn't take my fly on the Green because if trout had been around they had decided in their fishy way not to bite the fly. I was very stoned in a back seat of a car because I wasn't not stoned. I hadn't talked to my mother on the phone for a year because it hadn't occurred to me to do so. When Sylvia or Tim looked at me I was a person they had known only a short time, Sylvia seven days and Tim eight. It was so accidental and the force of it with the sprinkle of opium pushed me back into the seat until I became part of the Naugahyde. A plastic fantastic non-lover. If I happened to return to my wife assuming she welcomed me it would probably be for want of anything better or more interesting to do, or if I happened to be in the area when it occurred to me to try, or if she hadn't met someone else at a party or the grocery store. Things that were dead were not alive as surely as that bird dog I had grieved for several years. Her location was certain as I had buried her.

In Jackson Hole we had a good meal and I drank a whole bottle of Pinot Chardonnay because they didn't like the taste. After dinner we wandered around from bar to bar and Tim scored a quarter gram of cocaine off a guitarist during a break. I idly thought his money must be running out but rather liked the idea of a line or two of coke. But back in the motel it turned out to be weak and overcut. Despite this Tim was pissed at Sylvia for refusing to try any. I had picked up some magazines and Eastern newspapers so that when they went back out I decided to stay. I was pleased when Sylvia looked disappointed. I could tell she didn't want to go out either but hesitated to expose herself to whatever Tim might decide to say.

All the bars had resembled various movie sets and you couldn't tell the gimcrack from the real cowboys, not that it mattered. Why shouldn't a hard-working stockbroker from Boston be entitled to wear a costume once in a while. This reminded me of the more functional, nevertheless silly-looking, sailing costumes they wore in Marblehead and Martha's Vineyard or Vinalhaven.

I poured a glass of bourbon and settled back with my reading material. Mrs. Nixon had flown to South America to assuage the griefs of the Peruvians who had lost 25,000 relatives in an earthquake. The magazine said that that was more than half the number of our war fatalities in a single night. I puzzled over this as the comparison didn't seem apt. The Tigers weren't doing worth a shit. How often in youth they had broken my heart. All that I read was commonplace-sounding, even the earthquake which could not be translated from the print. I regretted not buying skin magazines.

By the time Sylvia came in I was low to the ground and had lost the precarious balance I try to keep when drinking. I heard Tim's car roar off and hoped he was gone for the night. She stayed a long time in the shower after a few pleasantries and in my near drunkenness I kept dozing off when I wanted to stay alert. When the bathroom door finally clicked I was totally awake.

"Why don't you just hop in bed with me." I had intended something smooth but my voice was both tight and my speech a trifle slurred. She walked past me and sat on the edge of her own bed. "Why don't you come over here a minute."

She looked at me as if I had just flown in from Tibet. "Can I have one of your sleeping pills?" she asked.

"They're in my kit in the bottle marked Valium. Only take one."

When she got back she turned out all the lights except the TV which rotated the weather forecast with the wind, humidity and temperature accompanied by Mantovani-type music. She stood there in a light flannel nightie letting me palpitate with cheap suspense. Then she got into my bed and I drew her to me with my breath collapsing. I kissed her and found that her cheeks were wet. Oh Jesus. Then she began sobbing in earnest and I withdrew the hand that I had instantly covered her sex with. I got up and drank deeply from my bourbon bottle until to the horrible music of her crying the lights in my head went out.

CHAPTER

13

THURSDAY was ominous. I sat there naked in an armchair with my skin tight from the cold. The empty bottle lay near my foot. I squeezed my eyes hard several times to counteract the pain that surged up behind them in continuous slow rolls. The window was open and Tim lay on his bed covers with only shirt and socks on. My own bed was empty but looked slept in and what had happened made its way past the pain and into my consciousness. On the floor beside my bed Mrs. Nixon was looking just over the top of my head from *Time* and next to the magazine was the short flannel nightie that had been next to me for less than a minute. We were no more than a day away from buying the kerosene and fertilizer and the sticks of dynamite needed to get it going and my dreams had somehow recognized this imminency by orchestrating all sorts of explosions which were conducted by my dead father. "Daddy I can't come to you, you'll have to come to me," she sang. Suicide would not be the problem today though. I was in for the sort of hangover that protects itself by striking out at everything: enough brain cells were dead so that the animal only thought of its own howling wounds.

It must be only fifty in here and the only sign of life is my hard-on, the boozer's friend, this morning diuretic erection. Saves marriages by making Mom forgive last night's sins. There was a powerful smell of bourbon in my mustache. We should blow up the fucking motel for not turning on the heat.

Tim sat up in bed and looked at me. "What's happening?" He was puzzled and glanced over at my bed.

"I got drunk and fell asleep here." I still had not decided whether moving was worthwhile. Even to get warm.

"I tried to get you into bed but you wouldn't move. Sylvia wouldn't say anything." He was rubbing his eyes and looked very bleary and bored.

"I wanted to have her but she was crying and it turned me off so much I drank the whiskey."

He looked sympathetic for a moment then got up. "It's fucking winter in here."

While he was in the bathroom Sylvia came in with coffee. She wouldn't look at me directly and I truly wanted to kick her in the ass. It was partly the hangover but it seemed that this morning I had finally lost all patience with her. I felt coldly analytical about the sexual barrier that had grown larger between us as if we had somehow missed our prime chance and this loss had driven the final queasy remnant of tenderness from my head.

"How's our little ole crybaby this morning?" She was looking over the top of my head like Pat Nixon on the floor behind her. I could see that she wasn't going to reply standing there pale and shivering in a light sweater and that short blue skirt. Her legs had goose pimples.

I leaned forward and stared into my coffee trying to invent some adequate torment. "You should go home. You're no use to anyone and the way you're acting you're liable to fuck up the project."

She looked down at me and I immediately was sorry that I

said it. I had no guts for meanness of the more dramatic sort, only for a long relaxed meanness by omission.

"I'm sorry I cried last night." She turned and quickly walked out the door even though I called to her.

We were quiet in the car and I brooded when we crossed the Snake River. I had counted on fishing it but the day wasn't much over forty and huge clouds were sweeping through and over the Tetons. It would be snowing up there. The Tetons always appeared as excessively pretty to me, not serious mountains but mountains created by a pastry chef for the wealthy ranchers around Jackson Hole. But I cautioned myself with the thought of what a prick I'd be if I owned ten thousand acres of that land and had the income to maintain it—maybe a Lear Jet to fly me to San Francisco for dinner, probably wander around the ranch clearing my throat like Melvyn Douglas and vote for Nixon. At cocktail parties I would say "We got to stop this goddamned runaway inflation" and my guests would be attentive because I was very rich and they wanted to be invited again. A frowsy wife would pipe up "Right on, Bernard, our savings are being eaten up like sixty" and I would smile and nod at her and think, That little woman has got some real horse sense. Then my wife would yell "Chow's on" and the whole party would lash into piles of prime beef and ranch beans and later we would all dance to stacks of Glenn Miller and Guy Lombardo records while all our children were smoking dope in Europe.

We were going over the top of Teton Pass with snow ticking steadily off the windshield when I touched a hideous nerve of failure in myself: Sylvia was right and Tim and myself were wrong. Or maybe. Or at least she was a part of that purportedly normal group that formed such a stunning majority. I saw us as goats who stood for alcohol, dope, dynamite, errant promiscuity, while she was some hearth goddess who was

sweet, virtuous, gentle, kind and faithful. It must be the guilt
that accompanies a hangover. And she was simple-minded.
The meanness crept in again. Tie her up and throw her over
the cliff on the left side of the car which was going too fast
for the slippery conditions. Or don't tie her up but send her
home. I wasn't used to questioning the essential truth of the
way I lived. My life might be a loathsome mess to an outsider
but I cherished the notion that it was honest. All lapsed Cal-
vinists continue to crave that simple monism by which everything is excusable because it is inevitable. "God willed it"
when one still believed, and after that, "At least I'm honest."
But now in the back seat my honesty seemed poor and thin in
the light of Sylvia's naïve altruism which, though battered,
daily centered in her wanting to wholly love someone and to
be loved as totally and faithfully in return. That was certainly
asking too much on earth from my own experience—if adopted
as a guiding plan it could very well tear your head off. For me,
anyway. It could work for Sylvia but not with Tim and much
less with someone like myself who was so falsely battle worn.

Of course she wasn't as simple as I was pretending, but
nearly. She had swallowed the whole bait and now it was be-
traying her. She merely waited. And was punished. And there
was no real majority of the sane to be a member of. She had
gradually by the act of waiting for Tim cut herself off from
all but a few like Rosie and Frank and her mother whom she
exchanged letters with and now on the road sent so many of
those postcards that look like nothing at all on earth. And her
mother whose marriage had been and still was awful and dim-
witted didn't really care any more that she wasn't actually
married to Tim. After the initial shock many parents nowadays
accepted the fact that their children were simply living with
each other. A decade before and it would have been unimagi-
nable. Fathers had visited daughters and met the friends of
daughters and had come away after saying their piece with a

niggling desire to get some action themselves, or a regret that they had been so deep in their post-Depression haze that they forgot to have much fun. So the clarity got by my hangover began to diffuse and wander. Whether or not I would be good to Sylvia meant nothing to me when weighed against my desire for her. There were no mysteries involved: I would love her but I doubted if that would cure me any more than it had Tim. I wasn't diseased. I was the disease perhaps. And my pretensions toward admiring myself on this brutish level were as nasty as any other form of cancer. If I did any good at all it might be to let a few miserable fish swim to that higher, cleaner water where they were surely meant to spawn, as surely anyway as we are meant to die or vote or drink or screw out our torpid days.

There was an odd lot of freakishness in what suddenly began to happen. I was engrossed in a pile of maps when Sylvia yelped. I looked up to see my side window aimed at the center of the road with the car still going very fast. Then the road came at the back window and I thought that we were backing up terribly fast. We must have switched ends a half dozen times on the icy road and when we came to rest in a dip I discovered that I was yelling at Tim something on the order of "You stupid jackoff, you goddamn hillbilly freak." By mutual wordless consent we jumped out and faced off for a fight but Tim started slipping when he stepped from the shoulder onto the pavement and made a neat little skater's pirouette. My balance was less fortunate—I went down hard on my ass and if I hadn't thrown my arms behind me I would have cracked my head open. It was that ugly sharp pain of having a chair pulled out from under you and I doubted sprawled there on the glazed road in a thin film of snow that I would ever walk again. I lay back and looked straight up at the flakes that seemed to aim at my face and veer off at the last possible moment. A few made their target and melted.

"Are you all right?" Sylvia knelt beside me and slipped a hand under my head. Tim took my hand and pulled me into a seated position.

"Get me the whiskey." I felt horribly undignified and Tim was giggling. "We'll have to postpone the fight for a few hours." He trotted along the shoulder and then whipped out on the ice and twirled around in a tricky maneuver. Then he came back down into the dip whooping and giving us the finger as he passed.

"Do you want to try to stand up? You'll get wet there." Sylvia handed me the whiskey and I took a huge gulp, caught my breath and took another.

"You know that asshole was going too fast." Now Tim was way up the hill behind us launching into a run for a super effort. He came past us at a startling speed this time with both index fingers raised. I only thought he would be easy to hit with my sixteen-gauge Remington Model 12, say with buckshot or a simple slug through the middle. Sylvia made a little run and lost her balance but came down easily on her hands and knees. I crawled over and pulled myself up by the door handle. The feeling had returned to my legs but my ass still hurt badly.

We made our way slowly down the divide with two tires on the shoulder and when we reached the valley it was noticeably warmer on the western slope. I lay back to ease my discomfort and returned to my maps. There would be some trickery involved in getting Tim over to the Big Hole River where I wanted to fish but I remembered he had mentioned Chief Joseph in Key West and the scene of the battle was close to the river. But he probably wouldn't notice the circuitous route and his accrued knowledge about Indians had been got from Zane Grey novels and the movies. *Cheyenne Autumn* had disgusted him. Also, the Seminoles were pitiful to him and a Choctaw had been in his battalion in "Nam" as he called it.

"You're missing the scenery." Sylvia leaned over the back seat to check on my health.

"Fuck the scenery." What was left of my pain was gradually being displaced by the whiskey. I looked up over my maps. "Just describe it and I'll decide if it's worth looking at."

"Sylvia, you do a job on that poor old boy and it might cheer him up." I could tell from the sound of the motor and the sway of the shocks on curves that we were back up to our habitual ninety.

"I think he's hurt too bad." She leaned over and patted my head. I took her hand and began kissing it then licked between her fingers. She withdrew her hand and raised her eyebrows. "It's sure he'll never do it again."

"I'll bet a thousand dollars on me," I said. My brain was on a pool in the Big Hole I had fished several years back. Maybe the salmon flies would be hatching. I hoped that it would be too early for the main part of the runoff which usually came in mid-June. The Green had been fine, maybe a little too high, but if the runoff had begun in earnest the Big Hole wouldn't be fishable. "By this time tomorrow we can be looking at the dam."

"About goddamn time," Tim said.

I felt less enthusiastic. If I only had broken my back . . . but then I saw myself swaddled in a body cast with Sylvia definitely out of reach by reason of plaster. Wounded. She sits by the hospital bed with some lilacs she has picked. There is music of course. She locks the door and takes off her clothes but I am a male plaster manikin and nothing is possible. She weeps.

"Let's eat." The car swerves off the road onto gravel and stops. Tim gets out and starts to help me.

"I'm O.K." I find that I can hobble but my thoughts are back in the hospital room. I craved to be with her alone so badly that my throat ached. Throughout an awful meal we discussed our plans. We would get the fertilizer, kerosene and U-Haul in Missoula. There was no point in a trial run when we could experiment with a dam.

But my mind was dully on Sylvia and I wanted to be with her back in that shabby apartment in Valdosta. I would take her to the Keys with me. Or anywhere. Maybe we would have children and become thirty and forty together. But I was disturbed remembering that long pull of boredom in marriage, that "love" as I knew it didn't hold enough energy or velocity to hold interest after three or four years in my own experience. But my own peculiar mania had cut down on my resourcefulness. So much nastiness involved in earning a living. And once or twice a week you would have to stop at a gas station for fuel. Very small matters like gas stations were capable of causing a sort of paralytic hysteria if the timing was off. In the last month or two of my wife's pregnancy I did all the grocery shopping and supermarkets exceeded service stations in horror. Nothing looked good to eat. I would wander the aisles nearly weeping I wanted so badly to find something good to eat. It made the clerks nervous—there were a few murmurs of "weirdo." Mad Hatter goes shopping but there was nothing funny about it.

The worst explosion of all, the one that precipitated the breakdown oddly enough centered on fishing. At a family meeting attended by those who loved me and wanted to help I announced I wanted to own a fishing tackle and sporting store. I hadn't previously thought of such an idea but I was cornered and was in a bad bargaining position having just lost my third job of that year. The two sets of parents jabbered tolerantly about the idea while my wife sat in the other room watching television. I kept glancing at my watch having arranged to meet a friend for drinks and a pool game. I didn't get my store but a job was arranged for me in the "outdoor" department of a large department store to see if I proved effective in the line of work. Never have I suffered so. My few fishing and bird-hunting friends were a charming and literate group. But the people who came in to buy the junk we carried or to buy fish and game licenses were collectively less charming than a drunken bowling team. I sort of knew this before I started work but I wanted to make good. I organized a beautiful fly display case but no one bought flies and no one bought the marvelous fly rods I had ordered without permission. The manager kept saying "I told you so." And there were complaints. A real estate salesman bought a case of shotgun shells and told me in passing that he had shot seventy crows the day before. I always have had a soft spot for crows. My comment was a loud "You must be a real asshole." And on the licenses it was fun to reduce the height and vastly increase the weight of the buyer. They always lied anyway. It got so bad that the regular customers avoided me and I only got to let loose my spleen on the unwary. Everyone looked like a murderous blimp. And I said so.

CHAPTER

14

I SLIPPED out of the cabin in the total darkness about an hour
before dawn. There was an owl in the trees on the hill behind
the cabin that I had been listening to and now in the moonlight I hoped to catch a glimpse of him if he began chasing
something. Barely enough moonlight to make out the watch
dial and at the appointed time I nearly didn't get up, the bed
was so warm and the air cool though there was no bite to it.
I gave up on the owl who obviously had been disturbed by
me and poked around in the car gathering my tackle. I sat behind the wheel and ate some sharp cheddar and crackers but
the cheese had been bought two days before and didn't taste
very good. I dismissed an urge to wash it down and supplant
its rank taste with a sip or two of bourbon. Sitting there in the
cool dark I felt more conscious than I had in the previous eight
days and I rather liked this unexpected awareness although it
took some effort to push out of my mind that dam near Orofino. It was only a hundred and fifty miles to the northwest but
during the night it had seemed right outside the door. Time is
running out. And butterflies were fluttering in my bowels and

brain and whiskey had no power to diminish them. Not far out there in the dark was the Big Hole River. The night before when we pulled into Wisdom I shined my flashlight into the water from the bridge and saw that it was clear enough to fish. Now I dozed a minute or two with my forehead against the steering wheel.

There was a trace of Sylvia's jasmine scent in the car so I got out. Shocking like the effect of smelling salts when I was knocked out playing football. I did not want to think of her while I fished but the odor in the dark of the sage and sweetgrass and pine resembled a subtle perfume and I was drawn to her despite my desires to the contrary. I had listened to her breathing and liked the way it intermingled with the hooting of the owl and a very distant sound of a whippoorwill. Now I could see a faint edge of light over the slope between Odell Mountain and Alders Peak and I began to walk to the river.

There was a strangeness to the morning that disturbed me and at first I attributed it to the similarity of walking to the river as I had walked to so many rivers on so many dawns. A car approached at high speed and I stepped off the blacktop into the grass I had been avoiding out of paranoia over rattlesnakes. As the headlights swept past and the car bobbed in the dips of the road I could hear music from the radio and it took several minutes for the sound and the red taillights to disappear up toward Chief Joseph Pass. Maybe that formed a little of the strangeness. Less than a hundred years ago Gibbon's men had crept leading their horses here up to the Nez Percé encampment. An old brave probably out taking a morning leak had finally seen them and his eyesight was reputed to be bad. The first bullets caught him anyway and then the Cavalry charged the sleeping tents.

I reached the bridge and dimly made out the narrow path down to the river. When it got lighter I would walk downstream for a mile or two and then fish back up. But I wanted to be able to see a path. The snakes' rattle was their way of saying they didn't want to be stepped on. I had so little of what I thought of as courage. It was easy enough to suppose that courage was somehow mixed up with energy and your metabolism; I knew that it was unlikely that Tim ever backed down from a fight or the danger of competitive driving, and when he did make some comment about the war, fear never entered the language. And blowing up the dam seemed as simple to him as having a meal or going to a movie, even simpler than the act of screwing which he apparently had some problems with. And the Nez Percé who had battled on the ground where I stood had a saying when war was near—"Take courage, this is a good day to die"—just as the Miniconjou Sioux had said "Take courage, the earth is all that lasts." Eerie to be able to say such a thing and mean it.

Now it was barely light enough for me to make out the shape of the entire Big Hole basin which was some seven by fifteen miles. It was once a high summer pasture for elk and bison and in the blurred and dulcet light of early morning it was possible to believe it still owned that virginal state. The water had a strong even flow and I had had good luck within a few miles of this spot but now the ground fog that curled and drifted across the sage hung above the river. Fog or heavy mist always disturbed fly fishing as insects tended to avoid it and there was nothing for fish to rise to. I tied on a streamer, a minnow imitation, and began to cast but I couldn't concentrate.

Gibbon's men had watched the squaws come out of the tee-pees and stoke the morning fires before returning to their husbands and children. Then the old half-blind brave who was the first kill. Then the charge with the Cavalry shooting low into the tents to pick up as many sleeping bodies as possible, which was a rather usual Army strategy in those days. Fifty women and children had been killed. Even babies. No Nez

Percé sentries had been posted as this sort of attack wasn't in their own repertory and they were trying to evade the Army anyway.

I had a sharp heavy strike but failed to hook the fish. I moved along the bank further to try another hole feeling very bad that I had begun to think about the Nez Percé. Outrage was the most vaporish of emotions. It occurred to me with some amusement that a student in the future might have his grade dropped on an exam from a B to a C because he mis-guessed the exact number of My Lai dead. The water re-minded me of the name of Chief Looking Glass. I looked at my reflection in the water and said it aloud several times. He drank water here. Funny how such errant details make it real as if my own reflected body were that of Looking Glass taking a drink a few minutes before the battle. The Nez Percé had regrouped quickly and had killed some thirty of the Cavalry and wounded forty. If you could except the squaws and chil-dren which you couldn't they would be the clear winners. When Gibbon's men finally withdrew after twenty-four hours the Indians traveled on and those who pursued them found along the trail some wounded and aged who voluntarily dropped out in order not to impede the flight. Gibbon's Ban-nock scouts got their scalps.

I took several brown trout, none of an interesting size, but as the first bit of sunlight burned away the fog, insects began to appear and trout rose to them. I could see the dim-ples and circles of rising fish down to a bend where the river disappeared in a grove of willows above which the mist still hung. I had no stupid urge to be here when it was unspoiled because it was nearly unspoiled now. It was hard on your brain finally to have to think constantly of searching out a place that was relatively "unspoiled." But you could reach an incredibly primitive area of the coast of Ecuador and find that the black marlin in that infinite Pacific had nearly all been lost to the Japanese longliners who cherished them for fish sausages.

I had certainly been born too late to cream it and I knew how resolutely fatuous it was to blow up a single dam. Or fifty or a hundred. But I felt almost sure that it would make me feel good and however primitive and silly that reasoning was it would have to do. I knew that I would have given up in Arizona had it not been for Sylvia and this admission made my holy passion suspect. It was simply a good idea but I was just as simply not geared to carrying it out on a large scale. While I was fishing I could feel the ebb and flow of my reasoning almost with every cast and retrieve, and it was only momentarily interrupted by watching a large brown trout swirling against the far bank. I begin to think of Sylvia waking and how my courage for even this small but elemental battle was weak. I almost wanted Tim to reconcile himself to her though I knew this was unlikely. I fantasized through a dozen casts that they would vanish while I was fishing. I would pretend to be shocked and, at first, getting over Sylvia posed some difficulty but this might be resolved by hiking up into the mountains, perhaps way over into the desolate Selway-Bitterroot area of Idaho. Who would cook my meals? Horseshit. Ideally I would climb one of the surrounding mountains, mistake a lightning bolt for a power vision, and die with my charcoaled body blasted into a crescent smile. Locals would call the mountain Big Smiley. An anti-legend might be formed including choice information: at fourteen his heifer took last place at the fair; at twenty-two he had difficulty staying awake; at twenty-six his wife asked him to leave but to please not take the car; at twenty-eight he climbed his first mountain and made a smile.

I had two hours of excellent fishing then and all other considerations were lost in the excitement. I even planned how I might attack the evening hatch and what part of the river was a likely alternative to my morning fishing as I wanted to cover new ground. I wished that I had a frying pan and some bacon and could fry a few trout quickly in the bacon fat or that Sylvia were sitting on the bank like a Nez Percé squaw ready to cook her brave's fish. How romantic. A sickness, actually. Pure and simple an unquestionable disease to which there were no alternatives this late in life. I could not help but assume it was late in life because I had no notion of what was possible next other than returning to Key West for a few weeks tarpon fishing after, of course, we had the satisfaction of blowing up the dam.

I hoped enough notice would be paid to the incident that I might collect a few newspaper clippings to show to friends. The barflies would be astounded. And fishing friends would admire me for doing what many fishermen thought of frequently. I deserved some of the same kind of praise that the Fox had been getting near Chicago only my debut in the realm of ecological violence was much more dramatic. *Sabotage.* The word lifted my neck hairs and made me shiver. I released a final trout and began walking back to the cabin. The fishing had slowed somewhat and we wanted to get up to Missourla to buy our unsuspicious material before the stores closed. And Tim wanted ammunition for the pistol which we argued over but then I remembered that small arms are popular in Montana and there would be no danger in getting shells. A few years before I had met a minister who enjoyed shooting rattlesnakes with his .357 on Sunday afternoons. It was relaxing after a hard morning at the pulpit.

I guessed it to be about ten in the morning when I let myself in the cabin door. I was quiet, then noticed with some disgust that Sylvia had her leg over Tim's hip. A pretty picture for a voyeur but the nature of voyeurism indisputably changes when you think you love the object. Tim had an inexplicable

bruise above his scar but it couldn't compete in interest with
Sylvia's ass. That's not just plumbing, I thought, but I had to
squint so Tim's nudeness didn't vitiate Sylvia's. Odd to be
homosexual and be only interested in the other. I tiptoed past
the sleeping bodies. Tim always had to have the bed closest
the door, a mania he got overseas. Not to be cornered, taken,
and eat rice for years in a bamboo cage. I took a shower and
crowed loudly a rendition of "America," a song that tran-
scended its status as a nullity after my morning on the Big
Hole. Be nice to drive down the road a piece and receive in-
struction at the feet of Joseph himself. But he loved his
squaws, there were two of them late in life, and nine children,
only one of which lived long. He clearly wouldn't like me and
I didn't very much either. I could redeem myself in his eyes
easily enough by blowing up dams. Fish were a staple for the
Nez Percé.

When I got out of the shower they were still there but Tim's
eyes were open and Sylvia's legs were close together and
drawn up fetally. Her body somehow raised the question of
suicide. An abyss safe from harm's way.

"Well you missed it last night." Tim stretched his arms and
yawned.

"I see your face. Did she hit you?" She still hadn't wakened
and I thought how silly it was to stand there making conversation when I ought to be shooting him and jumping her. In
Granada I once had mistook a wife for a daughter and there
was a lot of fleering Spanish passion that was only resolved
when I lost face and left the taverna. Should have kicked his
face in.

"This bugfucker grabbed her when I was dancing and when
I grabbed her back he hit me. So I drilled the motherfucker."
He held up his right hand and the knuckles were ugly and
swollen.

"Must have been a good punch."

"A great punch. He was drunk and they didn't even cut me off."

They had gone to the only bar in Wisdom for something to eat while I had walked down to check the river. I stopped by for a nightcap but the only thing to eat other than pickled bologna was XRAYE SANDWICHES, CHUCKWAGONS AND CHILI DOGS. The food was placed in a small aluminum oven and within a few minutes the buzzer rang and the food was ready. There was a group of wrangler types at the other end of the bar and I thought I overheard some slighting reference to the length of our hair. Tim either hadn't heard or pretended not to—I knew he wouldn't let such a comment pass. He and Sylvia danced two numbers while I had my drink and now it seemed that it had been plainly an enticement to the cowboys what with Tim's habitual sneer and Sylvia's short skirt. I thought I had had my mind on the river but I probably subconsciously wanted to avoid a hassle.

Tim got up to re-enact the scene. Good fighters can always shadow-box with such speed that you fairly hear their fists whish through the air. I was suddenly happy that our ice-skating fight in Wyoming had come to nothing.

Then Tim put his arm around my shoulder. "Pretty close to zero hour, huh?" He laughed and walked to the bathroom.

I blushed. I wasn't used to nude men putting their arm around my shoulder, plus I thought it was a tacit accusation over my leaving the tavern when I knew secretly that a fight might be inevitable.

Sylvia woke up and made no move to cover herself. We had become not nature's children but familiar people whose concerns were too ill and fractionated to care about our bodies.

"Sylvia, cover up or I'm going to fuck you right now." I sat down next to her on the bed.

"Timmy knocked this guy's teeth out." She rubbed her

144

sleepy eyes and stretched. I leaned over and kissed her belly button. "I was afraid they would gang up on him and almost ran over to wake you up." I moved my mouth lower in mock trial. "Don't do that." She tried to push my head away.

"Why?" My question was muffled against her sex.

"Because!" She jumped up and drew the sheet to her in mock alarm. I could hear the shower running and felt safe. I advanced on her and put my arms around her but she was play-acting and put on a mincing show of the seduced.

"Sylvia, goddamnit." She let me kiss her once and I was hard against her and almost thought I was home for a moment. Then I got that same "please" again and sat down on my own bed with my head in my face. I thought of rape. Tim would only think it was funny but she came over and began rubbing my neck and shoulders.

"It's not what you're thinking. This isn't a good time." She had anticipated some foul question that I intended to ask or state about the night before. I drew her tightly to me for a moment then let her get dressed. Tim came out with his hair slicked back like Mifume and laughed when I tried to cover my embarrassment with my hands.

CHAPTER

15

IN THE CAR moving toward the vast line of the Bitterroots I
began an odiously boring lecture on Indians. At first they listened civilly with the tape deck turned low, not knowing that
I had dropped one of Tim's spansules to try to ameliorate my
growing dread which had got totally out of hand. How in
Christ did he take so many of them when a single one set me
off like an endless string of firecrackers. And not that I really
knew much about Indians other than what I remembered from
LaFarge and a few other books in high school but I countered
my ignorance with what I thought was eloquent invention. I
characterized my favorites—Nez Percé, Cheyenne, Blackfoot
and Mandan, maybe the Oglala Sioux. I kept on through the
switchbacks on Chief Joseph Pass, embellishing each doubtful
fact with mystery. Sylvia turned on her seat and faced me so
I increased and exaggerated the romantic aspects which of
course in reality were few. I had meant to take a Seconal and
sleep, not an upper. Sylvia's arm trailed over the seat and I
could barely hear Dylan on the deck; my voice grew an octave
higher and was on the verge of quacking. I should own a duck
ranch, a harmless spread speckled with ducks. After we killed

the ducks and shipped them to the cities we could make duck-feather pillows, assuming there was a market. How could I blow up a dam when I hadn't ever voted, a comparatively sane political act? Sylvia and I would go to the polls together then stop at Burger Chef. She was partial to Burger Chefs and though I despised them compromises are essential in marriage. We would grow tired too of eating duck. There would be no pills on the ranch and only the mildest strains of grass would be allowed. Wine, not whiskey. The children could have a duck or two to play with. Sitting on the front porch she would say the ducks have been good to us this year. I might have to tell her to shut up.

Tim had turned the music up when I lapsed into my duck silence. I speculated that I could flit around the mountains like Road Runner escaping the coyote. If I closed my eyes I saw an enormous billowing orange explosion and a towering geyser of water and mud. Then some Navajos stood looking at the site of their sheep shed. Where's our sheep shed? Little Face saw it blow up and a red car escaping. My temples pounded. What ever happened to Gene Krupa. I opened my eyes and rolled a large joint assuming that it would counteract the speed better than alcohol. If it didn't I could always try whiskey later. I handed it to Sylvia but she passed it on to Tim.

"It's too beautiful today." She was rubbernecking the Bitter-roots. But the statement appeared in the air as a judgment on me. I was irked anyway at having forgotten to take my vitamins in my haste to go fishing.

"Tim, Sylvia thinks these mountains are more beautiful than we are. I think that's inconsiderate."

"She always was corny. I asked her to send me a sexy picture of her and she sent one in a bathing suit. A bathing suit!" He shook his head. "By sexy I meant no clothes."

"You'd just pass it around," Sylvia said good-naturedly.

"They didn't know you. I see her naked since she was seventeen and she won't even send a picture while I'm protecting her ass in Nam."

I should have kept my mouth shut. Quarrels didn't serve to keep my mind off what we intended to do in the next twenty-four hours. They jangled. What quarrels I had had with women, week-long sullen wranglings like dogs parrying in a property dispute. While you're up get me a drink. Get it yourself, you're drinking too much. Fuck you. Don't talk that way in front of your daughter. She's not listening. Yes she is. She's watching Archie on TV. No she's not, children are upset by their parents' voices when they're cross. Then get me a drink and shut up. No. I'm going out. Don't take the grocery money. And so on.

I had Tim stop when we crossed the West Fork of the Bitterroot River near Conner. I felt compulsive about my vitamins and needed water to get them down. We sat and talked in an addled way about an escape route while Sylvia waded along a shallow stretch of the river with the announced intention of finding a gold nugget. Tim thought we should double back into Montana at least as far as Bozeman. We were pulling the kind of stunt that local authorities would naturally suspect of Californians and maybe we would drop a key ring with a California address on an ID tag. It sounded like a barbershop crime magazine trick to me but I agreed. I wanted to contribute something crafty to the plot but couldn't come up with anything.

We sat there with a pint of whiskey watching Sylvia sort the rocks and ask us which we thought might have some gold in them. I pretended I knew, saying igneous and ultracrutaceous. She was so placid and believing, and today especially she looked much younger in the knee-deep rushing water. She deserved a small farm and a horse to ride on or something like that. At age twelve in Sunday school the teacher told us to treat and regard all girls like little sisters. I felt sappish and cold-headed with Tim talking very intensely about details while I for the hundredth time in eight days so envied him his woman that it was unbearable. An idle mind. You have a job in order to be so bored that you are kept out of mischief.

Maybe Joseph stopped to water his thousand horses here while the Cavalry from Fort Fizzle were in pursuit. Fort Fizzle! The actual name. Look it up. Soldiers from Fort Fizzle killed fifty of our wives and children. It couldn't compete with Wounded Knee but then it is difficult to see atrocities racing neck and neck for the atrocity championship. I used to love the Russians and was upset when Katyn forest was pinned on them. I didn't want to hurt anyone except myself, and an observation ward with small paper cups with pills forming a total jewel in the bottom wasn't an interesting alternative.

"Sylvia, you might go to prison." Why should she be girlish if I couldn't be boyish.

She looked up from a rock. "I don't care." The sun caught her hair and burnished it copper. In the shadow of her face her eyes were very green and happy.

"I'm not going to any fucking prison." Tim looked belligerent though the bruise had subsided. The knuckles on his right fist still looked skinned and raw. You dance around with a pretty girl in an absurdly short skirt inciting horny young drunks to riot then you smash in the face of the one who makes the first move. And you do it with enough authority to discourage the others. She's mine, jackoffs. The code of the South, and West. Part of the North. I'd seen many tavern fights with two louts whacking each other's face into hamburger. And Tim's "you'll never take me alive" attitude fit into the same code which was artificially inseminated a hundred times a year by the movies. Sylvia bent over for a stone and we were impolitely mooned.

"That doesn't do anything for me," Tim yelled. She turned and thumbed her nose.

"It does a whole lot for me." He pulled my ear but gently. I

wondered suddenly what he intended on earth. It was obvious
that we weren't looking at the same woman. He was liable to
call her skinny twice a day though I knew at five-seven she
went about a hundred twenty. But such tastes aren't arguable.
It was clearly familiarity—they had known each other closely
longer than I had been married but with the same lack of suc-
cess it seemed.

"Sylvia, he doesn't want you. Let's get married."

"You're already married." She was sorting the rocks for
keepers.

"We can get married now then I'll get a divorce." I was
painfully serious though a good measure of my giddy serious-
ness was the grass.

"I don't think either of you are worth marrying." She stepped
out on the bank where we sat and handed me her choices for
approval. I studiously turned the rocks over and over then
struck two of them together until they had ugly white scars on
their damp surfaces. It was pathetic that she was confusing me
with Tim in our non-race for her hand, almost insulting.

"I'll be the best man." Tim lay back and chewed on a stalk
of snake grass. "And I'll give away the virgin bride. She's so
good you'll want to cut off her head by the end of the year."

Sylvia shrugged and walked over to the car. I calmed down
a bit after thinking about what a drag it is to be understood.
There was a mosquito drowning in our whiskey bottle and I
squinted through the neck at his struggle. If I married again it
would be to someone who could support my fishing habits.
There's a hole on the porch of our house in Valdosta and we
have no money to buy a board. My fly rod is broken and we
must spend the two hundred dollars we saved for the baby.
The baby will have to be put off. Until never.

The main problem in Missoula proved to be the air which
was acrid and yellow from the huge conical lumber kilns and

stung the nose and eyes. It seemed ironical that the town was favored naturally by the confluence of three lovely rivers, was surrounded by mountains, was the learning center of Montana with its university, and still the whole place smelled like a stinking pile of shit which required an absolute mutation of the senses to live with.

We stopped briefly at a five and dime while Sylvia ran in and bought a key chain to be planted before we escaped. People were bustling around the streets as if they weren't breathing air that reminded one of a hog turd. Tim said it smelled like the remains of a Cong hit with the new super-stickum napalm. He said if the stuff hit you you could jump in a lake and still burn to death. When Sylvia came out we drove around looking for a grain elevator and ranch supply store in order to get the fertilizer and kerosene and the few sticks of dynamite needed to set it off. I reflected dully on how we could adjust to any conditions in where we lived or warred or even loved. Sylvia was chattering to Tim about the songs they used to like and again I was relegated to being a passenger. Spite. You were better off with women if you at least pretended you knew what you were doing. Being oblique and directionless is the least attractive characteristic if you want to get screwed. A moron will get layed a lot if he has the self-assurance of an average ward heeler.

I remembered the day at sixteen that I won the 880-yard run at an unimportant dual meet and with a mediocre time. But there were many students there because it was a fine spring day. I was laved in adoration for a week until my vanity became insupportable. I got bare tit with two different girls on dates—the movies were unnecessary, you just took them for a drive in your 1947 Plymouth. But then I placed seventh in the county meet on a beer hangover and vomited under the bleachers. And the girls whose udders I had suckled at, whose lips I had french-kissed and tasted their Spearmint tongues, would scarcely speak to me. A friend had won the 4-H three bottom plowing contest and had had a wonderful time for a week or two until he failed to qualify for the state finals. Tim had neither the essential brains nor the metabolism to ever question himself. Or from childhood he had never slowed down, thus women were attracted to his velocity. In so many slight encounters wherever we had stopped I had noticed it, whether it was waitresses, whores, bar girls or ranchers' daughters in Jackson Hole.

We picked up a small open U-Haul with a tarp at a Gulf station then found our other supplies on the west side of town. Tim stuffed his hair up under a high-crowned straw cowboy hat he had bought in Douglas. We sat in the car for a half hour —he didn't think I looked genuine enough. There was a slight breeze and on this side of town you were almost free from the bad air. I thought Sylvia was acting too gay so I decided I would bring her down a bit.

"Sylvia, I love you." The car was very hot and she pushed her damp hair away from her forehead.

"I believe you." We kissed very briefly. For the first time it occurred to me that it wasn't just language, that she did believe I loved her. I was mildly frightened. Jesus.

Tim came out with a burly type following with the case of dynamite and two ten-gallon cans which they filled with kerosene at a pump. We were parked against a cyclone fence which enclosed countless bales of barbed wire. Tim backed the trailer up and the man helped him load the fertilizer at the elevator dock. I stuck my head out the window to catch the sweet grain smell which I loved. I used to like to stand in the wheat in my grandfather's granary in my bare feet. You would sink in halfway up your shins. The mice would be rattling around and swallows would peer at you from their nests along the beams. We reconnoitered in the car and agreed that there was no chance to reach Orofino in time to case the site that evening.

But we would have to drive that far and somehow arrange to be there close after dawn so we could figure out exactly what we would have to do.

At dinner we were all in good spirits. We stopped at a tavern south of Missoula for a sandwich but it was packed and the menu said WE SERVE CHOICE MONTANA BEEF AND REAL BUTTER. It was crowded with a mixture of miners, cowboys and businessmen. We played pool while waiting for the meal and I won twenty bucks. I thought the porterhouse steak was marvelous and aided by the whiskey I wanted to stay there forever. We took turns dancing with Sylvia who was very happy—she even got some scattered applause at which point Tim glared at those who clapped from the barstools. I decided I wouldn't walk out on this one but nothing materialized.

By the time we got back in the car I doubted our ability to reach Orofino that night and cared less. We had the tape deck up as loud as it would go and were singing with Tammy Wynette's "Divorce," a mournful song where the husband and wife spell out their words so that little Joe, aged four, won't understand that Mom and Dad are going to split. At Lolo Hot Springs we saw the signs and decided to take a bath in the springs. There were only a few cars in the lot and I argued with myself whether I wanted the hot sulfur water treatment or to go to the bar up the road whose neon lights I could see glittering so attractively.

The attendant seemed happy with our business and we separated to put on suits in the dank stalls. Tim poked his head in mine to tell me we were going to wipe out every fucking dam in the whole U.S.A. At the edge of the pool I noticed that Sylvia was wearing her crocheted bikini. Two couples were in the process of leaving and I prayed that I would never get fat and white like the men. We soaked in the springs which were somewhere over body temperature. It was an effort to paddle around and I thought of falling asleep and drowning.

Tim didn't like it and got out telling us to meet him at the tavern down the road. He said he had to drive and the hot water tired him out. The springs were open air with the wood bathhouse surrounding them. I floated on my back staring up at the stars, realizing I didn't recognize a single constellation. I swam over to Sylvia who was resting with her elbows on the edge of the pool. She asked me if I thought everything would go O.K. tomorrow and I managed an "of course." I kissed and nuzzled the back of her neck and pressed myself to her. She turned around and we began necking in earnest but it was difficult to keep above the water's surface so we moved slowly to the shallower end of the pool. The music they piped in was terrible but we ceased noticing it. I knew that she was fairly drunk but then it occurred to me that she might, like myself, be acting more out of control than she really was. I sank in the water and pulled off the bottom of her bathing suit and waved it at her while she laughed. I reached down to make sure I was there and glanced around to see if the attendant was there. I was and he wasn't. I suddenly felt terribly sober. She put her arms around me and lifted her legs. I moved us into the yet shallower water and kissed her as I entered.

CHAPTER

16

WE STOOD in the water caressing each other while I told lies.
Then the attendant came and told us he wanted to close for
the night, by which time I wanted her again. Walking up the
road to the bar I tried to hold her hand but she would have
none of it and any questions I asked went unanswered. It all
seemed so casual and abortive, so terribly brief and unlikely,
and not what I had planned at all. As we neared the tavern I
began to get depressed and drew her to me with force. I had
guessed that she was crying but that was far away and unimportant: I wanted some signal of permanence to have been
made by our lovemaking, no matter how ludicrous it had been.

"Don't tell him," she said against my neck.

"Don't be silly." I was weighted down then by my own stu-
pidities, the hundred things I had said to her or in front of her
that might make her believe that I'd create a joke out of it. "I
love you. I won't tell him." But the word "love" sounded flimsy
and childish from my mouth.

"There's no way to be with each other." We were leaning
against the car and through the screen door of the tavern we
could hear Tim's voice, then a pause, then laughter. Her state-

ment was an announcement of fact and there wasn't any doubt in her voice. "You're just like him and I couldn't go through that again."

I began to deny this but she turned and walked up the steps and through the tavern door. I smoked a cigarette and felt a kind of palpable sleaziness that I hadn't known in years. Perhaps I was like him. I thought of myself as much smarter but that made no difference to her or to me for that matter. I stood there trying to pull from airy nothing, from the exhaust of the passing cars, some real difference between Tim and myself that I could use to assure her that my love was solid and that I would take care of her. But I couldn't and I never really intended to. I wanted to have her for a year. Or less. Though often in the past few days I believed I couldn't live without her there was the real question of whether I cared about living at all. Now standing there I felt a chill in my head that made all questions of what to do moot. I dreaded facing Tim. A transference of ownership. There were no safe places from her any more than there were safe places from the act we planned tomorrow.

In the bar I felt oddly murderous. If I got in a fight tonight and lost I would take the .38 from the glove compartment. We sat there on the barstools drinking tequila. Tim had a map of Idaho spread out and I pinpointed the location on the North Fork of the Clearwater in case I fell asleep. Sylvia was acting splendid. Maybe she felt that way but I could perceive in her no sign, no recognition of what had happened. I danced with her clumsily and went into a raving fit when a local tried to cut in. I got an apology but I could see Tim grinning over the guy's shoulder waiting to place the proper boot in the spine. I knew in my drunkenness that I had lost any remnant of control and would somehow merely have to wait and see what I would do.

They woke me up near Kooskia for coffee. My head hurt and

I had awakened intermittently hearing the clanking chains of the U-Haul and the loud tape. It was nearly two A.M. on the cafe clock and I figured us to be about sixty miles from the dam which was northwest of Orofino. I was tempted to forget but knew there was no way to get away with it. Tim was impossibly keyed up and it was infectious. We could case the situation right after dawn, then keep hidden during the day and pull our little number in the evening. Sylvia was in a semi-doze over her coffee and for a moment I felt cruel toward her sleepy vulnerability. Wake up. Don't just sit there like a cow until it's over. We had to drive a half dozen miles on a gravel road, then cut off on a two-track before we reached a ranch house. It was an even mile if I remembered correctly from the ranch house to the dam and the small lake or backwater that it created. When I had fished there the owner was up for the weekend from Boise and I doubted that he would be there this early in the season though I knew there had been at least one hand staying there all the time.

I felt bleary but strangely intent on what we were doing. Sylvia said she wanted to sleep but it was only two hours from dawn and if we got settled in a motel it would cost us another day. It had begun raining when we got back in the car, first small droplets then a steady downpour that made the driving difficult. I sat in front with Tim and while I gave him directions I kept thinking of the rain as a bad omen. Maybe the dam would wash away by itself with this amount of rain added to the melting snow of the spring runoff. How lovely. Sylvia lay curled asleep in the back and I could only see her legs. It was hard to believe that they had encircled me not a few hours before. Our bodies had felt very cool in the night air above the water. Perhaps it had happened last week.

We missed our turnoff the other side of Orofino and had to backtrack. But after several miles on a gravel road I saw the mercury vapor yard light in front of the ranch house and then the cattleguard and gate. I hoped the gate would be locked and when I unlatched it in the rain I thought of telling Tim that it was locked but turned to see him watching me between the headlights. We drove another mile down the rutted two-track and then pulled over into a clearing near a fence. It was too dark to hide the car but I was fairly sure there was no one at the house. Perhaps a neighbor only kept an eye on the place but I knew there were cattle. Tim was extremely edgy and we were on the verge of arguing several times. Within an hour he had finished four bottles of Coke and dropped two pills. I asked for a pill because I felt like a wet stone sitting there in the steamy car watching Sylvia's sleeping legs. And we had re-hearsed so many times that there wasn't anything to talk about until it got light and we could look over the dam.

"This is great." He turned and punched me in the shoulder and sorted through the tapes that lay in a jumble between us. "This is really a goddamned great thing we're doing. Shake." We shook hands and he popped in a Haggard tape that I was sick to death of.

"Maybe no one will hear it." I hopefully figured it was three miles from the nearest occupied house.

"You'll hear this son of a bitch ten miles away." He slapped the dashboard loudly and Sylvia awoke.

"Are we there?" She looked out the wet black windows and then at us. Her voice was bleak.

I closed my eyes and listened to the lyrics of "I Can't Hold Myself in Line"—the singer was mournfully going off the "deep end" because of love and whiskey. It was painfully accurate and I wanted to turn it off. If I turned away from Tim I was able to imagine that I was fishing and just waiting for the first light to make my way to the river. My father had always liked being near the river for a full hour before it was light enough. He would drink from a Thermos of coffee and smoke cigarettes wondering aloud about the weather and what stretch he might fish.

"What will we eat today?" Sylvia brought me back to the car.

"Each other, stupid." Tim thought this was a wonderful joke. "I bought a bag of junk while you guys were fucking in that hot water."

"Timmy!" Sylvia poked him in the ribs but her voice was playful.

"Don't Timmy me, I saw you. I bought this stuff," he said lifting a paper bag from the floor and shaking it, "and then came back and went in but you were fucking so I went back to the tavern."

There was an awful silence. Though the car was dark and the only sound was the rain and the metallic crackle of the engine cooling, our presences were so luridly real that we may as well have been shouting. Then Sylvia began a sort of dry weeping as if she were having difficulty with her breath. I reached over and gripped Tim's wrist as hard as I was able in an effort to get a message through. He caught.

"Jesus, Sylvia, I was bullshitting. I never left the place. Go to sleep and we'll wake you when it gets light." I withdrew my grip, wondering if he had actually seen us, not that it mattered as long as he assured her that he hadn't. He put his hand on my shoulder and then changed the tape. "That fucking Haggard makes me sad."

My eyes were open but I didn't notice the pale light coming through the trees until Tim got out of the car and stretched. My trance had been involved in trying to summon up enough good things that had happened in my life to ease my immediate fatalism. Despite the buzz of meth I was stuck to my seat again and my brain only lightened when I thought of how

Tim reassured Sylvia just an hour ago. It had seemed out of character.

The first order of the morning was to hide the car. We walked a few hundred feet further down the trail and found a hollow in a stand of spruce. The rain had stopped but the ruts in the trail were slippery and full of water. The air was incomprehensibly sweet and we could hear the roar of water coming under the conduit chutes of the dam but couldn't see the dam itself in the dim light. Tim backed the car and trailer in the spruce and we broke branches off and covered both the car and the bright orange trailer. Sylvia was humming and we were all in a good businesslike mood. Then we walked the hundred yards or so down to the dam itself and I was appalled: the dam was at least seventy feet across and about twelve feet wide. There was a cattle path and tractor tracks across the top of it and it looked terribly solid. The backwater stretched until it was lost in the morning fog; and underneath the water passed through three conduits a yard in diameter shooting out with tremendous force onto a declining series of rock steps. A quarter mile downstream I could make out the North Fork of the Clearwater. I was stunned both with the size of the dam and the momentum of the water. Tim walked the cowpath studying the setup and we followed with Sylvia folding her arms against the chill.

"Shore is a big bastard." Tim was drawing on a scrap of paper with a ballpoint. He stooped and held the paper against his knee. I noticed for the first time that he had the .38 stuck in his belt.

"I think it's too big for what we got." I only remembered glancing at the dam in irritation when I had seen it a year and a half before. It hadn't seemed nearly so large. On the bank of the backwater was a huge irrigation pump and large pipe used to irrigate pasture and hayfields. The soil was porous and wouldn't hold the rain long enough for a good crop of hay.

"No, we got plenty. We'll just have to place it right." Tim slid down the bank on the downstream side to get a better look at the structure of the conduits. He yelled something at us but it was lost in the din of water. I felt a very giddy itch to get my rod and walk down to the Clearwater which I could see flowing hugely along between its banks of rock and pine.

On the way back to the car we were startled by noise in the brush and Tim, stupidly I thought, pulled out his pistol. But then a group of shorthorn cattle appeared and walked past us toward the pond. Three or four of the cows had calves and these turned and bellowed at us. I hoped it wasn't a cow-calf operation because they always included a seed bull that could be rather nasty, especially if they were range cattle and not used to people. We were nearly to the car when we heard the sound of a motor and literally dove into the brush and deep grass. An old Dodge pick-up passed within a few feet of us driving toward the dam. Tim eased his head out of the cover.

"It's turning around." We sank even lower to the wet ground. I idly brushed a mosquito from Sylvia's leg and contemplated moving my hand up her leg but thought it wouldn't be fair. I stifled a giggle; my minimal dose of meth was in full stride and I felt when the pick-up came back past us that I could jump out and kick it off the road like a toy.

"Maybe he just comes by once a day." Tim scratched his head and I saw he was sweating profusely. A drop trickled down over his scar which looked ghastly against his paleness. He hadn't been eating much unless he smoked a joint first and then it was mostly junk like hamburgers and potato chips and Coke.

We sat around in the car talking excitedly for an hour or so. I explained again how impossible it was for the steelhead, a fish they had never seen, to move up through the conduits to spawn where they had been spawned themselves and generations before them. I was rattling on when Tim decided to sneak

over and have a look at the ranch house to check for activity. I
wanted to go along but he said no, that he had had a lot of
experience. He put on a faded green fatigue shirt and left.

"We could make love." I looked at Sylvia in the back but
she returned my stare blankly.

"Don't be silly."

I got out of the car, pushed the brush aside and sat on the
hood. Oh well. I wanted to pass the time. I lit a joint and
smoked it down to a wee roach. I was thinking of the day a
few weeks before when on a dare I had dropped a triple hit
of psilocybin and passed twelve hours in a sweet trance. I
mostly sat on a pier and watched the movement of the tide but
toward the end I walked across town to a raw bar and ate
clams, oysters, shrimp and some smoked amberjack. There was
a delicious red haze tingeing all people and objects and though
I was terribly disoriented it didn't seem to matter. I went to a
girl's apartment and talked for a while and we made love, but
it was very hard to concentrate because I kept getting lost in
the music on the phonograph. Sylvia put her hand on my arm
and I was startled.

"Do you think it will work?"

I put my arms around her and kissed her neck and lips. "He
didn't see us. He was teasing." I enjoyed the lie because it obviously brought her happiness. I massaged her hips and then
pressed my hand tightly against her crotch but she backed
away.

"You're not getting me started again now." Her face was
flushed and smiling.

"Just thought I'd try. It wasn't very good in the water."

"It felt fine to me." She brushed a mosquito off her arm and
I tried to catch her but she stepped away. "Maybe we'll get
another chance."

I didn't hear Tim when he returned. I was sprawled dozing
uncomfortably across the bucket seats in the front but when I

awoke Sylvia sounded upset. I looked out at them standing against the hood. Tim had blood all over his hands and shirt and Levi's.

"What the hell happened?" I was sure he was badly injured.

"When that guy left he let a Doberman out of the truck. A watchdog. He won't come back for him probably until tomorrow. But the dog scented me so I had to kill it." He knelt and plunged the knife into the ground several times to clean it. The idea of killing a dog repelled me though I never liked Dobermans.

Tim took his scrap of paper off the dashboard and began telling me that we would have to place the entire charge near the center conduit. A single large hole would loosen the entire structure of the dam aided by the force of the water.

CHAPTER

17

THE DAY was passing at an unbearable crawl. By noon there had been eight hours of daylight and we would have to wait eight more to be safe. By mid-morning we had finished the sack of trash Tim had bought in Lolo Hot Springs: all the sort of food I hated—candy bars, pretzels, peanuts. I found the cheese I had eaten the morning I fished the Big Hole wedged in the back seat, but it was granular and so rank I couldn't get it past my nose. Out of boredom we finished a half pint of whiskey, the last of the alcohol. I mentally re-ate my porterhouse of the day before. Tim split a spansule of meth and we each snorted half: then we had an argument about whether it was safe for me to go fishing and I finally agreed that it wasn't. The day had grown warm and humid and Sylvia sunned herself in her bikini in a small glade back in the pines. While Tim went off to make further studies of the dam I sat on the edge of the blanket and tried to talk to her. I wondered idly if Chief Joseph might have taken a hunting party up this particular small valley. At one time his band of Nez Percé had owned three thousand horses. That made them very hard for the Cavalry to chase because the Nez Percé could change to fresh mounts at will. Sylvia lay on her back with her body glistening with Coppertone. Her sunglasses reflected the light like mirrors but I supposed that she had her eyes closed. I placed my palm on the middle of her tummy.

"Please don't." Her politeness goaded me and I pulled the bottom of her bikini down until my fingers were against the hair. "I wish you wouldn't do that." I pulled the suit down even further marveling at how white her skin was contrasted with her slight tan. "Timmy might come." She sat up and took off her glasses.

"He just left to make a diagram." I kissed her but she pushed me away and lay back down. I could still see the top of her sex and I quickly pulled the suit down to her knees. She stiffened. "Turn over." She didn't move so I rolled her over and pulled the bathing suit off her feet. I lay between her legs which I forced outward and kissed her until I could no longer bear it.

"Please hurry." Again the politness. But I was so maniacally excited that it didn't take very long. I quickly pulled up my Levi's and walked back to the car. I thought my heart would burst and my limbs were shaking.

At the dam Tim was busy with his tablet and pen. I took off my clothes and dove into the backwater but got out as rapidly as possible. The water was no more than forty degrees and I drank deeply as I surfaced. Tim's diagram was very elaborate but I knew he had had some training in demolitions. It would be bad indeed if very many of our disenchanted veterans decided to apply their knowledge. I thought of that building at the University of Wisconsin. Down at the mouth of the canyon above the Clearwater new thunderheads were building up. I dressed and we jogged back to the car not wanting to get wet. Sylvia only appeared after it began raining again. She said she had been asleep. I was on the verge of weeping when she got into the car. All my maudlin propensities temporarily overcame me. She wore Tim's mottled blue cowboy shirt over her bikini and her skin still shone with the suntan oil and its scent pervaded the car.

I had two joints and we passed one of them among us while Tim pointed out the subtleties of his sketch. Everything was running out. Sylvia announced that she had dropped the ID tab in the grass in front of the car. She sounded proud and conspiratorial. We rolled the windows up tight and started the car and heater because the rain and wind had suddenly turned cold. We smoked the second joint and went on a laughing jag. Here we were at the end of the road with not many hours before we would bring the whole wonderful thing off. We gibbered at one another and laughed hysterically over the silliest insubstantial jokes.

Tim admitted that he made a lot of money from fencing the drugs that he stole from the hospital with a friend, everything from Seconal to morphine to Demerol to Thorazine to ordinary Darvon. They peddled to patients at exorbitant prices. One of the patients had died but he would have died anyway. Sylvia told the story of her first date with Tim and how he was making love to her before she was even quite sure what he was doing. And I told the story about how I talked to a psychiatrist and assured him nothing was wrong with me when meanwhile I had torn the phonebook from his desk into confetti-sized pieces.

But then the sky got much darker though it was only midafternoon and the wind blew so hard that the spruce branches were swept off the car and trailer. The rain let up after a half hour but the wind was still violent and cold. Tim watched the weather changes closely and grew morose.

"We can start now." He got out of the car and began untying the tarpaulin knots on the trailer but came back to get his jacket.

"I think we should wait until dark." I exchanged glances with Sylvia but my worries vanished for a moment when I looked at her eyes which looked too close together a week ago but now seemed so flawless. I thought Tim was in a Seconal-speed daze and I wanted him to relax before evening when the real work would begin.

"No." He sat there staring out the window and it appeared he was very near an overdose or perhaps more depressed than I had ever seen him. But then just as suddenly his spirits picked up and we chattered for another fifteen minutes while Sylvia brushed back our hair and made pigtails with rubber bands from her purse partly because we didn't want the hair blown into our faces by the wind and partly because we decided to be Indians. She drew large rings around our eyes and mouths with lipstick and three vertical streaks on our cheeks down to our chins. We were very happy.

It took seven trips apiece to get all the fertilizer and kerosene and the case of dynamite to the dam. I was cold, wet and exhausted but Tim seemed to pick up energy with each trip. The sky had grown even darker and the clouds were rolling only a thousand feet or so above our heads. Sylvia walked along with us in my leather jacket which was growing dark and wet with the rain which had begun to fall again. I begged Tim when he started to dig along the conduit on the face of the dam to wait until evening but he said there was no point in it. There was a small roll of powder fuse and I thought of kicking it over into the backwater but was unable to move.

We were interrupted by the appearance of the cattle. Sylvia was frightened by one especially belligerent yearling bull who came halfway out on the dam swinging his horns and bellowing at us. I was frankly ready for a retreat but Tim ran at the bull with the shovel and smacked him hard against the neck and it ran off bawling. I felt stupid and cowardly again. I lowered the bags of nitrogen down to Tim who placed five on each side of the conduit. Then he clambered up the bank and we sat there smoking cigarettes with our backs to the wind.

The noise of the water was too loud for talk. We both had our hands on Sylvia's shoulders. On the far bank the cattle were watching us with studied curiosity and I wondered how we would get them out of the way when we set off the charge. I didn't want a cow on my bloody hands. Tim started walking back to the car and we followed. I somehow wanted a bigger part in what we were doing but I felt inept and nearly comatose. It was hard for me to believe that I was at a dam near Orofino, Idaho, and what's more was in the preparatory stages of blowing the goddamn thing to pieces.

In the car Tim was cold and abrupt. He took his pliers from the glove compartment and worked them nervously with a steady clacking.

"Sylvia, turn the car around and keep it going. And stay here."

"I want to see the explosion."

He paused a moment then nodded agreement. A string of cattle passed down the trail in front of us in the direction of the ranch. "Those fucking cows. I don't want to blow up any cows." The scar had grown more livid in the cold, wet wind: a faded blue laurel that the government would rid him of free of charge. "While I set up I want you to take the shovel and keep the cattle away."

We had walked halfway back to the dam when Sylvia called out to us. She had managed to get the trailer stuck in the ditch on the other side of the road. We had to uncouple the trailer and lift it out of the ditch. Sylvia murmured her apologies several times but Tim said nothing. I felt terminally disconnected with the way things kept going wrong: first the Doberman with the slit throat then the omnipresent cattle and now the stuck car. When we got it straightened around Tim stationed Sylvia about a hundred yards from the dam behind a big stump where she would be safe but still able to see the explosion. We giggled at how absurd our painted faces looked and Sylvia wanted to touch them up as it had begun to rain again and when we wiped the water from our eyes we smeared the lipstick. But Tim jogged down to the dam and I stayed just long enough to get my make-up corrected.

Tim slit open the tops of the fertilizer bags and rearranged them in the trench he had dug along above the conduit. I handed down the kerosene with a wary eye out for the cattle. He soaked down each of the ten bags and handed the cans back up to me and scrambled up the bank waving me away. I walked back and stood by Sylvia while Tim wrapped the sticks of dynamite in a bunch and placed it between the double trench of fertilizer. He worked on his knees arranging the caps and unrolling the powder fuse. I started back down the slope but he waved me away again and covered the setup with loose dirt. Ideally, he had said, the bags should be placed further into the wall of the dam but the base was made out of logs and stones and was impossible to dig through.

Tim signaled and I ran down to him.

"Take this back to the trunk." There was at least half of a case of dynamite left.

"We don't want to get caught with this." He nodded and picked up the case and threw it in the backwater but it floated. Then he threw in the spool of powder fuse and it sank. We had to shout to each other to be heard over the roar of water. There was a large group of cattle up on the hill and I wondered how they would get back after we blew up the dam. But the stream would probably be shallow enough for them to wade it after the backwater flowed through. I thought proudly that by tomorrow steelhead would begin making their way up past where we stood on their spring run.

"Well here we go." We shook hands and he punched my shoulder. I was looking down at the setup and the fuse didn't seem very long but I didn't know what its burn rate was. "Go up by Sylvia and keep your heads down."

I walked slowly toward Sylvia wanting somehow to think of a further delay. The cold wind depressed me and the rain stung my face. Sylvia's smile warmed me somewhat and I gave her a kiss. Then we turned to Tim who was waving. We waved back and Sylvia threw him a kiss. He raised his arms and clenched his fists together in the victory sign. Then he took out his lighter and held it to the fuse.

What I saw then at first didn't register on me I suppose because of the possible horror. The cattle were coming in single file down the path on the side of the hill and were heading slowly for the dam. Tim had just dropped the lighted fuse and had begun running across the dam toward us when he saw me headed toward him. He turned around and saw the cattle and ran back toward them pausing to stomp out the fuse. He took out the pistol and fired it in the air but the sound was puny and lost in the water and didn't dissuade the cattle. He picked up the shovel and headed toward them swinging it in a semi-circle. I began to head back to Sylvia when I noticed I couldn't see the white fuse which had been so plainly visible before. I knew suddenly that his stomp hadn't put it out. I screamed and waved. I saw him lower the shovel and turn from the first of the cattle, a cow and a calf, who were drawing closer. Then he looked down at the place the fuse should have been and started running. I reached Sylvia in a few seconds and her hands were covering her face. I stumbled and fell sideways. I saw that Tim must have tried to stomp on the fuse again because he hadn't cleared the dam when the blast came.

The first shock wave spun Sylvia around and seemed to lift me off the grass. In the great cloud of mud and water I thought I caught a split-second picture of Tim hurtling through the air but I hoped it was the calf. But the sound hit us in an all-encompassing deafening roar and the trees' limbs bent with it. I lay there as the mud and water covered us and I saw

Sylvia's mouth was open as if she was screaming but the blast had stunned my ears.

We got up slowly, then ran down to the dam with Sylvia ahead of me. A great hole had been torn in the middle of the dam and the backwater had begun to rush through and gradually widen the opening. The calf lay against the far bank covered with mud. Not far away the cow was moving forward on its legs which were badly broken. She collapsed on her stomach but still edged toward the bank on her knees. I ran partway out on the dam but felt the earth trembling under my feet. I could hear now but the cow was bawling out horribly and the water sounded like a freight train. I turned and saw that Sylvia was standing on the rock steps beyond the first conduit below me. Tim was lying on his face nearly concealed by the mud.

I jumped down the bank and slipped twice getting to her. She was kneeling beside him and had him turned over with his head on her lap. She was still screaming. I knew immediately that he was dead. Blood was coming from his eyes and ears and nose and in quantity from his mouth, and one of his legs was tilted at a crazy angle. I touched the leg but quickly withdrew my hand when I saw it was nearly torn from his body. I saw that the hole was growing larger in the dam and we would have to get out of there to avoid drowning. I slipped off his dog tags which he still wore and looked for his billfold but remembered he had left it on the dashboard. I tried to drag Sylvia away but she wouldn't let go so I hit her hard along the temple and dragged her up the bank and onto the grass. I went back to Tim and tried to lift him but couldn't get a grip on his slippery clothes. The pistol had slipped down into his crotch and I emptied the chamber on the cow to stop her bawling. I propped Tim against a rock and wrapped my hand around his collar and started pulling but his shirt ripped. Then I grabbed him by the pigtail and made some progress but the water had risen to my knees and I could see that the whole dam was on the verge of giving way just as we had planned. I looked down into his open eyes and saw how the rain was washing his face clean and the blood from his mouth had slowed to a trickle. There couldn't be much of it left. Sylvia was sitting up now holding her face in her hands. She looked at me and I shook my head. Tim's body was trailing off in the current held only by my grip on his hair. I let go and barely made it to shore before the water reached my waist. I avoided being swept away by taking hold of some willow branches that dipped downward to the water. I took Sylvia's arm and moved her as quickly as I could to the car. It seemed to me that I knew Tim would die the moment he turned from the cattle and looked in amazement at the fuse that was no longer there. And then he had tried to run in those gaudy blue cowboy boots. Sylvia was moaning and I kept telling her to shut up but found that I was weeping myself and that my ears still rang from the explosion.

I fishtailed the car down the trail narrowly missing going into a ditch. We made it to the blacktop, through Orofino and out to Route 12 without noticing any police cars. I couldn't seem to drive fast and keep the car under control with the trailer swinging behind so I dumped it in a park near the Selway River outside of Lowell. Sylvia was slumped weeping in the seat with her hands over her face. I noticed for the first time that her skirt was soaked with blood. We would have to find a place to clean up. In the rearview mirror I caught a startling sight of my face with the tribal stripes still intact.

EPILOGUE

I SOMEHOW expected roadblocks by the time we reached the Montana border but nothing materialized. The rain had become a violent thunderstorm and I began to wonder if our handiwork would be discovered at all or perhaps was confused with a thunderclap. But I couldn't remember what I had done with the pistol which couldn't be traced further than Douglas, and the trailer had our fingerprints on it. And Tim's body might not be found for months. I felt sure I would eventually be caught but was unsure how they might go about it. This sort of spring deluge could knock out a dam I thought. Would the cow and calf be washed away? As we drove on in silence with the storm roaring about us my thoughts were drawn to the bluffs along the Yellowstone near Livingston. I could drive out on them, get out, slip the car in low gear and watch it disappear in the river. Or even better I could drive it to Chicago and either abandon it in a ghetto where it would surely be stolen or leave it at a parking lot at O'Hare and remove the license plates. I was frankly interested in saving my skin. Judges and ranchers in Idaho were not likely to look with mercy on sabotage and dead cattle or murdered watchdogs.

Then there was the impossible problem of Sylvia who broke the silence with an occasional sob that made me jerk involuntarily at the wheel. We did not speak until the other side of Missoula. When we passed the hot springs near Lolo I had squeezed her arm but only got more weeping for my efforts.

"I'll put you on a plane in Bozeman." No answer. My throat was constricted enough that it was hard to talk. "You go back home and I'll get in touch with you. If we get caught there's no point in you being involved."

We drove another fifty miles before I got an answer. I put a tape in but pulled it right back out—the music sounded awful and implausibly tinny, almost blasphemous. I stopped on the banks of the Jefferson on the other side of Whitehall and washed up and changed my clothes. We needed gas and I didn't want to stop at a station caked and smeared with a combination of mud and lipstick and blood.

"What can I tell his parents?" Her voice was small and tight.

"Say that he drove to Alaska. Or was going to Africa. Or Mexico. Something like that." Tim's death became more present and immediate. When I got back in the car after cleaning up I saw the blood on her skirt again, a nearly black stain that covered her lap. Alaska. If there weren't so many dams he would float down the Clearwater to the Snake to the Columbia and out into the Pacific. But a snag from a log would catch him or he would sink then float after a few days in the backwater of one of those huge dams that dot all the major watercourses of the West. They have fish ladders for steelhead. I have seen the strong ones make their laborious way up a three-hundred-foot incline. All to spawn where they themselves were born.

It was nearly midnight when we stopped at a motel near Boseman. Before she went into the bathroom I gave Sylvia three ten-milligram Valiums to dull her misery a bit. I walked to a bar down the road in the lessening rain and had a half dozen doubles as quickly as I could drink them. When I got back she was in bed with her face turned to the wall. I called the airport and made reservations for her to Atlanta with connections through Chicago for ten the next morning.

It would be a long night. I added some Valium to the whiskey swilling in my stomach. She sat up in bed and called to me and I sat down beside her and took her hand. Then I lay there fully clothed waiting for the drug and exhaustion to put her asleep. Every time I closed my own eyes I would see either the bawling cow or Tim cleaning his knife or his body floating away from me in the current. I imagined she was seeing much the same thing and I wanted to take her in my arms but thought it would be misunderstood. But then she collapsed against me and I hugged her while she wept. I stared at the ceiling watching the lights of the passing cars and trucks flicker across the ceiling and the far wall. I thought of trying to say something to comfort her but my brain had become wordless. Who would miss Tim besides Sylvia? And perhaps myself. For a moment I thought of blowing up more dams to honor him but doubted I could carry it off. I knew that in a very direct way I was responsible but felt nothing. I wanted him back. And what would Sylvia do now? It seemed unlikely that I would see her again after I put her on the plane. Maybe I should go home a few days and say hello in case I did get caught and sent to prison for a few years. But that seemed unlikely too. An act that I had conceived of as heroic would probably go unnoticed except by a rancher who might wonder why his dam had never washed away before, or why his Doberman was dead, or why he was missing two of his cattle. Two dead and two missing. My shoulder was wet with Sylvia's tears by the time she slept. My mind circled itself into a black, sleepless knot but I felt oddly alive. Suicide wasn't the question. For an hour or so I lapsed into fantasies of fishing. I caught an endless succession of tarpon until my arms were tired but Sylvia had pressed against my left arm until it slept. The first light eased through the window. I looked down at her bare breasts and then closely at her sleeping face. I kissed her lips very lightly and she stirred but slept on. Someone should take care of her but if I had any qualities of kindness and mercy left, any perceptions of what I was on earth however dim and stupid, I knew it couldn't be me.